Drawing Down The Moon:
Poems and Stories 1996

Drawing Down The Moon:
Poems and Stories 1996

edited by Robert Minhinnick

seren

seren is the book imprint of
Poetry Wales Press Ltd
2 Wyndham Street, Bridgend,
Mid Glamorgan, Wales CF31 1EF

A CIP record for this title is available from
the British Library Cataloguing in Publication Office

ISBN 1-85411-155-8

Cover painting: Storm Fragments with Crescent Moon
by Harriet Richards

Printed by The Cromwell Press, Melksham, Wiltshire

Contents

Introduction

Glyn Jones died this year. His death ends a literary era. But in the north, R.S. Thomas maintains his prodigious output of new work. In the south, Dannie Abse follows a more abstemious regime. Life was ever such: long may it continue. But in the middle, so to speak, things are stirring. This collection, first of what hopefully will be an annual series of new work by Welsh writers in English, hints at some of the changes.

The most obvious development might not be at once apparent from this collection. It is the demise of verse as the chief art form of English language writers in Wales. *Hallelujah!* I hear from various cynics. For too long, too many Welsh writers have believed that the short lyric and prosodic effusion propelled by personal neurosis or cultural paranoia, are the best, most necessary forms of expression, or that traditional verse forms should serve traditional political ends. The adoption of this position was made easier, perhaps inevitable, by a publishing scene that until fairly recently worked against fiction writers, essayists, biographers, dramatists, critics, and maverick cultural inquisitors. Poetic utterance, sometimes profound, sometimes puerile, but generally workmanlike, was too common.

The irony is that today more people are writing 'poetry' than ever before. Yet there is the distinct impression that there are fewer poets around. Most old hands are aghast at the poetry of the Welsh magazines, awash as they are with the outpourings of creative-writing course 'trained' versifiers and furiously workshopped middle class English incomers. The 'community' of writers that magazines like *Poetry Wales* once nurtured, is shattered. Although this might in itself be a very good thing, I am disappointed at not identifying more young writers, born or brought up in Wales, who demonstrate a degree of talent or originality. In fact, it seems to me that we have few visible writers born between 1955 and 1970. In England, Scotland and Ireland such people are already publishing. Speaking to one of the judges of a recent 'under thirties' poetry competition in Wales, I was told that overall the entries were disappointing. But as I have stated, this might signify healthy developments elsewhere.

And perhaps I am describing the situation too conventionally. It could be argued that the next literary comets will emerge from the

Internet or the home desktopping world and not the pages of some
literary journal. Also, it is probably pointless now to look to the old
spawning grounds of English language Welsh writers — Glamorgan
and Gwent — for the talented newcomers. It is feasible that our new
English writers will be bilingual, from Gwynedd, Clwyd or Dyfed.
Moreover, many of the authors whom we today classify as 'Welsh'
were actually born and brought up outside the country. It might still
be argued, however, that English-speaking Wales is under-achieving
in the creation of new writers.

Nevertheless, we should remember that writers under fifty years
of age here are usually considered either young or promising.
Occasionally both. After fifty, such people become fixtures, and
their output largely taken for granted. It flows on, occasionally
honoured but largely unscrutinised. There is an artistic, as well as
social, wisdom to this. In the wake of Dylan Thomas, young writers
in Wales have been treated with suspicion. They have had to prove
things slowly, especially to a conservative critical establishment, and
a university English department culture which in its present
wrestlings with post-structuralism, deconstruction and the baffling
genies of post-modernism, has made itself irrelevant to the worlds
of both writer and reader. In the critical vacuum created by the
departments, it has been Welsh historians who have read, inter-
preted and championed such writers as Alun Lewis and Gwyn
Thomas. The trouble with this school of criticism is that its texts,
composed by writers who were unique and possessed of individual
and difficult things to say, have been perceived as barometers for
social and historical change. Such writers wielded scalpels. But their
words have been appropriated and used as blunt instruments to
make historical points.

Such lack of critical attention is possibly one reason why Welsh
poets now develop in other genres. For instance, the poetic sensi-
bility Duncan Bush brings to the urban suspense novel provides that
form with unexpected qualities. Nigel Jenkins achieves similarly
surprising results in his recent work of historical rediscovery. As I
have said, this determination to work in areas beyond the tradition-
ally poetic is to be welcomed. But it could still be claimed that the
situation is depressing when compared to the Welsh language scene,
which despite its obvious problems, possesses a degree of real
excitement: for instance in the powerful links between poets, some

of whom work in the ancient strict metres, and contemporary rock and 'world' music.

On the other hand, in the UK overall, literature has become a supermarket perishable, overpackaged, doomed by its own sell-by date. This has been brought about, of course, for the reader's convenience, and as a method of combating the all-powerful visual media. It is not going to change. In Wales, the worst examples of the above are less in evidence. But there are other things to ponder. First we must study if only to reject the statements by senior Welsh male writers that distinctive English language writing here is a thing of the past. In a post-industrial Wales, bereft of much of the industry that created its urban culture, where the entire nature of work has radically altered, and which is beginning to sample the Prozac-like effects of the global media explosion, this seems at best simplistic and at worst self-serving. The notion that writing in English is only culturally valuable if it demonstrates a residual (or greater) influence of *yr hen iaith*, or if it defers to the traditional iconography of Welsh life, is worse than banal. It reveals an incomprehension of the energies of this country. Political correctness comes in many forms, not all of them malign. But like any uncreative orthodoxy, it is the enemy of meaningful art, as some of the work of writers as socially incorrect as John Tripp and Harri Webb reveals.

This said, what is distinctive about English language Wales is far more vulnerable to the homogenising impact of the almost-upon-us 500 Channel Universe than its Welsh language equivalent. (Though doubtless poetry, like Texas line dancing, child pornography and 24 hour coverage of the goings on in a Welsh *senedd*, will all have their own buttons on the remote control.) Moreover, the Internet and computer technology will exert new influences on our community lives. Yet there will still be a Wales, Welsh books and Welsh readers. That some might feel such a Wales is not worth reading about or writing for is pointless to debate. Every culture harks back to non-existent golden ages, and for many middle-aged and older people, the present (whenever it occurs) will always appear as some kind of betrayal. Such people, well respected, occupy influential positions in both English and Welsh language society. Yes, life in Wales was ever thus, but then literature, like the environment, has always had its doom-tellers.

Indeed, a greater threat than even the 'dumbing down' attitudes of American entertainment which now fill our TV and computer screens is the sentimentalization of our cultures by our own people and institutions. Cultures die when they turn their own mythologies into commerce. For example, Welsh rugby is mediocre in part because the Welsh insist in trading on an archetypal sentimental vision of the game and a primitive belief in an innate, supposedly mystical ability to play it better than other people. Industrial and 'heritage' tourism is a major growth industry in Wales — another decline into national sentimentality. The poetry of the sixties and seventies — the literary 'nationalist' era — is foxed by similar weaknesses. The poems of R.S. Thomas escape some of these because the author is desperate enough to reveal the hatred, pure and powerful, that impels his art. Writers such as Roland Mathias, John Ormond, Alun Richards, Ron Berry, Dannie Abse and Anthony Conran produced significant work because they avoided the nationalist clichés coined by contemporaries. Likewise Gillian Clarke, Duncan Bush, Steve Griffiths and John Davies of a later generation.

What are fascinating now, ironically, are the creative opportunities provided by a Wales gradually deciding that a greater degree of independence could not possibly be worse than sixteen years of valueless Conservative rule, or the creative coma that a Labour Party-dominated national and local government would induce. People in Wrexham, Rhondda and Pembroke Dock do not need to be 'nationalist' to understand that the way we live now is both undignified and insupportable, and that only a free or significantly 'freer' Wales will ensure the long term survival of distinctive English language culture here. Such political changes should have a tremendous impact on all our arts. Thus we need confident writers for the challenges ahead.

And thus to *Drawing Down the Moon*. I am delighted here to reproduce a significant section of the prose poems of Anne Szumigalski which first appeared in *Rapture of the Deep* published by Coteau books of Canada in 1991. Anne Szumigalski was born in England but lived in what was rural Denbighshire before an eventual move to Saskatchewan. She maintains a profound interest in things Welsh. Her delight in ideas, in intellectual games and the uses of myth, and her notions of poetic form have a good deal to teach writers in the UK, beset as so many of us are by anecdotal and descriptive habits. It is salutary to note how in this anthology her contributions loom out as wholly individual. Her work should be more widely available. It seems to me that Hilary Llewellyn-Williams is now producing poems of a confident richness, and I am pleased to present a goodly assortment here. Glenda Beagan is a challenging short story writer, and John Davies a poet whose work has not received the critical (or popular) attention it merits. But what is most noticeable, perhaps, is the absence of young (under thirty-five) writers. I could not find any but wish to have it proved that I did not seek hard enough. As it is, this collection boasts poems from Leslie Norris, Dannie Abse and Anthony Conran, none of whom might wish to be reminded of how long they have been making contributions to books like this.

Hopefully *Drawing Down the Moon: Poems and Stories '96* will be the first of a series. It could well be that the next anthology has a completely different authors' list. But whether this occurs depends as much on a belief in the existence of a distinctive literary culture in English-speaking Wales, capable of producing stimulating and entertaining work, as it does on establishing a readership. (Yes, there was a distinctive English language poetry in Wales in the sixties. But that does not mean we should take its literary merit for granted.) I believe that distinctive culture exists today. And as to whether *Drawing Down the Moon* fairly reflects what is now being written in Wales — that is up to you to decide.

Robert Minhinnick

Dannie Abse
Useful Knowledge

Shy Colin, the most silent of men
despite his ammunition of facts.
He'd bomb them out at dinner parties
before signing off from conversation.

'The mastrich tree, as you probably know
is brown, resinous, and most fragrant.'
'Volapuk? Nobody speaks it now.
Lost its one thousand, five hundred words.'

At Anne's, he said, 'Tortoises often die
from diphtheria.' At our place, he told us
'Lake Titicaca's half the size of Wales —
half's in Bolivia, half in Peru.'

Last April, when his two year old son
lay big-eyed in The Royal Infirmary,
Colin heard the consultant whisper
to his Registrar, 'Nieman-Pick Disease'.

Colin closed his eyes, cried out shrilly,
'A genetically determined disorder
where splenectomy is palliative.
Death occurs early during childhood.'

The Maestro

'I'll portray you with flutes, oboes and harp.'
So Schumann to Clara. As I would you.

Now in this front room of a tree-repeated street
I practise mere stumbling tunes. But the maestro
behind me, in the mirror, my discreet double,
plays your music's parables flawlessly,
Schumann-like, strange and tragical and sweet.

John Barnie
Up and Under!

Spider Davies sits on the pavilion veranda looking down the length
of the park. The wooden bench, he knows, is painted blue, though
he can't see it in the dark. It must be gone one o'clock, getting on
for two. Tuesday morning and Spider's drunk.

— Pissed outta my skull you mean.

Death's waiting there in the shadows of the veranda, though he's
not particularly rushed.

And the King definitely doesn't think suicide a good career move
at this stage.

— Spider. Spider. Cheer up. We'll squeeze a few more years out
of your liver yet. You're only forty-four. Everything to play for.

— Piss off King.

Spider gets up heavily. Steps forward out of the deep shadow at
the back of the veranda, to lean heavily on the smooth wooden rail
of the balustrade. Looking out over the park edged with orange
street lights.

— Not much of a life, he says out loud to himself.

The King and Death are listening.

— Not much of a bloody life.

He looks at the tennis courts in front of the pavilion. Spider never
played tennis. At school he left that to the prats from Western
Avenue and Chapel Road.

But he did have to play rugby, and on that playing field just the
far side of the courts.

— UP AND UNDER DAVIES! UP AND UNDER! AGH,
WHAT'S THE MATTER WITH YOU BOY!

— COME ON SCHOOL!

— WELL PLAYED JENKINS! WELL PLAYED!

And Jinks makes like he didn't hear this bit of praise from Mr
Jones PE. But he did and it makes him warm inside. He's already
one of the boys; already got a jock-strap-full.

Just as Spider didn't hear what Jones PE said too.

If thoughts could kill, thinks Spider, Abergavenny would be a
graveyard by now.

— Come on, says the King. It can't have been that bad.

— Can't it, says Spider.

— TWO-FOUR-SIX-EIGHT WHO-DO-WE-APPRECIATE KAY-AITCH-GEE-ESS SCHOOL.

— I never did hold with formal education, says the King. But good lord, you're a young man. Put the past behind you. You've got everything to live for. It's the future that counts.

— What future, says Spider. And in any case, what if you can't shake off the past because the past is what you are. What if the present is just the latest edge of the past riding out into the future.

Maybe some time way back changes could have been made. Maybe even at that pissing school. Though it was probably too late by then.

— Don't they wash behind the ears in your house Davies?

— Sorry Miss? What do you mean Miss?

— The back of your neck is filthy.

Standing in line at assembly while Mrs James inspects us; just passing the time of day until The Head, The Boss, The Pig comes in.

Nobody daring to turn to look, but all of them pissing themselves.

Afterwards she caught me on my own and said she was sorry; she shouldn't have said that in front of the others.

— Yes Miss. Thank you Miss.

— All right. Off you go.

And she smiled at me as if she was sorry for me rather than sorry.

Yes, the present is just the past trying to get an edge on the future.

— Too deep for me, says the King, stirring on the bench in the shadows. He can see the three-quarters empty bottle of vodka shimmering faintly beside him. The King feels thirsty after all this talk.

— Do you mind if I?

— Go ahead.

And the King unscrews the cap and takes a long hard draught — glug-glug-glug-glug. Ahhhh. Would you? Holding the bottle out.

Spider doesn't answer.

— Might as well finish it, then.

He drains the bottle and throws it over the wire netting into the tennis courts. It lands with a thud in the grass.

— Game, set, and match, says the King.

He sighs, then is moodily silent.

— Look, we've got to resolve this one way or the other.

— Do we, says Spider.

UP AND UNDER! I SAID UP AND UNDER! WHAT'S THE
MATTER WITH YOU BOY!
— COME ON KING HENRY'S!

The Unbelieving Soul

— You ever heard the tale of the Unbelieving Soul? That was Tyler
Grant. I don't remember him, he died a long time ago, but my
Daddy saw him when he was a boy and he told me the story.

Tyler Grant was a bad man, he always carried a .44. And in his
day he killed many-a men, you know. But it was always one of us.
He didn't mess with no whites, and so they let him alone.

Everybody was scared of Tyler Grant in Friars Point along in them
times, except one man, and that was Peetie Clayborn, old Reverend
Clayborn's father. He was a reverend too, and one day, so Daddy
says, he met Tyler Grant out near Caxton's Bottom. Along in them
times that was what you say, new ground, you know, hadn't never
been cleared. And Tyler Grant had been in there huntin. He came
out of the bottom with his huntin rifle, but he hadn't shot nothin.
And Reverend Clayborn's daddy went right up to him on that road
and looked him in the eye. Say, Tyler, you oughtta repent and start
prayin before you die. And the way the Reverend told it afterwards,
Tyler Grant just stood there for a while. Didn't say nothin. Then
he said real slow, Clayborn I ain't fixin to die. I'm gon live for
ninety-nine years. And I don't think you want to spread your wings
and fly to heaven awhile yourself, do you preacher. And he looked
through Reverend Clayborn like he wasn't there, brushed past him
like he hadn't noticed him, you know. The Reverend said afterwards
he felt like he'd been talkin to a ghost.

Well anyway, a week or so later they found Tyler Grant on that
same dirt road round by Caxton's Bottom, almost on the same spot
where Reverend Clayborn's daddy said he oughtta start prayin.
Spread out there in the dirt with a bullet wound in his head. It was
a heavy calibre bullet alright enough, probably a .45 so Daddy said.

It went in just above his right eye and blowed out the back of his head.

Well didn't nobody want to mess with that body. Because they was scared of Tyler Grant even when he was dead. So Reverend Clayborn's daddy say, Well uh, he can't be buried in no holy ground because he died in sin, but say, he got to be buried. Now who's goin to help. And nobody said anything, you know. Say, I know you're scared but someone got to bury him. Now who among you is it gonna be. So then my Granddaddy stepped forward. I'll help you Reverend. And the two of em walked off, hitched up my Grand-daddy's mules to his waggon and went on out to Caxton's Bottom.

And there he was out on the dirt road, flies crawlin and buzzin all over his face, in his nose, on his lips, over his eyes. Tyler Grant wasn't a big man, but it seemed like he weighed twice what he should, you know. Like his body was still full of sin, and it was weighing him down.

And they drove him to the edge of the bottom and found a place and began digging. In turns. They kept it up until it was almost noon. Say — Reverend I think we should stop a while. Let's do that. They were sweating hard by now, you know. And they found a tree and sat up in the shade, while the mules hung their heads, standin in the trees, and those big old flies buzzed and crawled up and down Tyler Grant's face, like they was devils searching for his soul.

So anyhow, after they'd rested up, they started to digging again and finished that hole, and drug Tyler Grant's body over to it and tipped him in. Shovelled earth on him fast. Then they covered the grave with brushwood and drove on back to Friars Point.

That night Reverend Clayborn's daddy wrote that song, The Unbelieving Soul. You ever heard that? They don't sing it much now, but for a while it was real big with the Sisters in the Amen corner, so Daddy says you know. 'All you got to do is be-lieve in Je-sus, Be-lieve in Je-sus, All you got to do is be-lieve in Je-sus, Not like that un-believing soul.' That's how it used to go.

So anyway, that was that. And after a few weeks nobody talked about Tyler Grant anymore and how he'd been killed and who had killed him. Until that November someone saw him for the first time, down in Caxton's Bottom. Tyler Grant's soul, wandering among the trees in that old swamp down there. Movin quickly, then stopping like he'd seen something, then movin quickly from tree to tree in the gloom.

I seen the Unbelieving Soul, they'd say, yesterday evenin down in the bottom. And it got so people wouldn't go that way after the sun went down, you know. Or Soul. I seen Soul last night.

They said he was so evil the Devil wouldn't have him in Hell. Say, Well-uh, you can't stay here. So there he was, the Unbelieving Soul, wandering from tree to tree down in the bottom. Nowhere to go.

But they say he never did cry out or come up to you or try to harm you. He just wandered round in the bottom there, movin fast then stopping, like he was looking for something, then found it; but no, that wasn't it, and after a while he'd be movin on. Like he couldn't remember but couldn't forget.

Nobody round here seen Soul in a long time. Though my Daddy seen him once. Just a white sort of glimmeriness running from tree to tree, just like they said.

There was a time, for a long time after Tyler Grant's death, Saturday night at the juke joint, everybody be laughin and having a good time. And someone'd come in, say, Look out! Soul's comin! I seen Soul comin down that road! And that place would empty. Wouldn't be a soul left in the place. So Daddy says, you know.

The Loneliness Room

— The trouble with Big Roger, said the man, is that he walked into the loneliness room.

The boy had been playing with his cars on the floor near the man's legs and large polished shoes. It was warm in the living room and still, except for the occasional ticking and rush of air bubbles as they fled through the pipes of the central heating. The boy loved this time of day, the curtains not yet drawn, and the fading light still good enough to see his cars on the floor. Outside a blackbird sang for a long time in the dying day, ending in an explosion of alarm cries. In the silence that followed the boy could hear the gurgling, splashing sound of wine being poured into a glass on the table above his head. He went on playing.

— He should never have done that, the man continued. He might have been alive now.

The boy didn't know what the loneliness room was, but he thought it must be out in the forest where the wine bird nests in spring. It must be in a hut deep among the trees that you stumble on by accident at dusk when you're lost. There'd be no lights, no sign of anyone, the boy decided. And the door's not locked, so you knock then push it open and tiptoe in. And there's a bed in there and a table and chair. No curtains on the window. You sleep on the bed and next day you wake up at dawn and look out of the window at the surrounding gloom of the trees. You go out. 'I'll walk all day now,' you say. 'And I'll find my way back home.' But at dusk what you think is a path leads you back to the hut, and it's just like it was before. Next day the same. Next day same again. And you're trapped. You realise there's no escaping the loneliness room.

— Roger always came last. Last in the mile race at the school sports, still lapping the track when the winners had been congratulated and gone off to the pavilion. Jeered on by us all. Come on Rodge. Come on Fatso. And one time old Percy Porter told us not to do that because Roger might not be a runner but at least he was a trier and entered into the spirit of the thing. It shut us up, and I admired Percy for that, but inside we didn't believe him. And Roger would puff by, face red as burgundy wine, fat arms and legs pumping, with a wobbly smile and a wave as he stumbled on. We couldn't shout, after what Percy said, so we made our hand-clapping sound like a jeer.

Always last, except in this one thing. Roger was the first one of us to enter the loneliness room.

The boy stopped playing, resting back on his heels, hands on his knees, listening to the man. He could hear him pour from the bottle again.

— No particular reason why it had to be him. Not necessarily Big Roger, though it had to be someone. Someone has to be in there. In Roger's case it was a question of the last shall be the first, for a change.

We didn't take much notice in the beginning. He'd always be in the bar when I arrived — this is years on now after we'd left school — sitting on a stool at the bar, laughing quietly at someone's joke, speaking quietly if he was spoken to. Not bothering anyone, sliding his glass across between the pumps for Ernie to fill it up. No words exchanged. Ernie knew what he wanted, and Roger knew the price.

Except the price was mounting. He started to leave about nine. 'Give us two flagons of Strongbow to take out, Ernie.' And he'd slip out of the swing doors with their old-fashioned frosted glass, so quietly half the time you didn't know he was gone. And we thought no more about it. It was his pattern now. Taking drink back to the loneliness room.

Later we heard it was gin or vodka at the off-license. Two flagons from The Pandy and a half bottle of gin from down the road. Landlords and shopkeepers always willing to help, doing their best. 'Certainly Roger.' And they'd be at the funeral later too, at least Ernie would. Standing round waiting for the coffin to come out of St Mary's into the sunlight. 'Well he's gone.' 'Aye.' 'He could put it back, could Roger, but I never expected this, I'd never have said he was an alki.' 'He could hold his drink.' 'But it got him in the end see.' 'Aye.' 'Bloody fool.'

Back in the loneliness room Roger would have known in advance what they'd say out there in the April sunshine waiting for the coffin to emerge. They'd all been there before. But he wouldn't have cared. 'When you're dead you're dead,' that was Roger's thought on mortality. And it meant nothing compared to that little hiss of escaping gas when you opened a flagon. Like an involuntary 'Ysshh' when someone puts a cold hand on your naked back. And the glug-glug-a-lug as the clear yellow of the Strongbow leaps and bounds over itself to get into the glass. The still and sparkling, eager, ready-to-go liquor, hissing slightly, the bubbles a release of celebratory balloons. A liquid leopard. Drink it down Roger. One long sip, head stretched out, lips suctioned to the edge of the glass. A second long sip. Head back for a third. Ahhh. The pint sleeve is empty. Another one? Aye why not. And for a nightcap what about a sip of gin.

Roger getting up fumble-eyed. Forgetting the room for the moment, that he always came back to.

— I don't like the loneliness room, says the boy.

— No of course you don't.

— When I grow up, I'm not going to go there, ever.

Glenda Beagan
The Man from Kurdistan

'Oh, but I couldn't do that', she said. 'No, really. I just couldn't.'

And briefly, searingly, I'd seen the dangers of fiction. Not for the first time, but freshly, somehow. Again I remembered all those old fears about writing.

Her frank and very blue German eyes made me squirm a little.

There were seven of us. All women. The youngest in her late thirties, the oldest pushing eighty, maybe. We sat round two tables pushed together in a cream painted room that had once been a chapel schoolroom. A cheese plant soared in the corner, a brief and early tribute to unlikely sophistication. A handwritten notice on the wall told us in Welsh and English that we were forbidden to imbibe intoxicating liquors on the premises. Beyond this, the table and the basic stacking chairs, the room was bare.

The building was the undoubted centre of life in this big scattered village but as we sat there, pens in hands, papers blank before us I wished that we were not next door to a huge discount food store. The warehouses were massive. All day long lorries would come and go. As they reversed out of the large yard they would *beep beep beep beep* constantly. Sometimes it sounded like an orchestra of lorries was tuning up for a big performance. It was not conducive to encouraging our creative efforts at all.

But Helga had been busy.

At the last meeting she'd handed me a thick exercise book chock full of her meticulous handwriting. It was a thoroughly worthy effort, especially bearing in mind that she was not writing in her first language. It gave an account of her life and was for the most part competently written but somewhat dull. Sadly she'd skimped on recording her childhood because here there were nuggets of brightness.

In the years immediately following the war the young Helga had gone to stay with relatives in the country. The writing suddenly took wings. There'd been an old house, a castle almost, with cellars and corridors and strangely shaped turret rooms. There'd been a dried moat full of coppery beech leaves where the children played and hid.

'This is marvellous,' I said. 'It's special and it's different. Can't you give us some more of this?'

'But that is all there was,' said Helga.

'Fictionalise, then,' I said. 'Invent some episodes. Enlarge on this material. Tell us a story, Helga.'

And then came that prompt disavowal. I felt rebuked, as though I were out to corrupt her, steer her away from the clear if common-place truth into the dubious realm of make-believe. To enlarge, to elaborate, to conjure up new elements would be wrong in her eyes. This was Helga's experience. It was true. It would remain inviolate.

'*No, really. I just couldn't.*' she said.

★   ★   ★

I'd noticed him on the station at Crewe.

There we were on platform eleven in the milling winter crowd and there he was laden with khaki backpacks and bedrolls. It was the earring I saw. It was elaborate, like a small version of those hanging lamps you find in churches sometimes. Or a censer, maybe. It was filigree silver. And it certainly took my eye.

I didn't stare though.

Later, (the train was leaving Chester by now so where had the earring man been in between?) the harassed looking girl with the refreshments trolley asked whether madam would mind if this gentleman sat beside her.

Well yes, madam did mind. Quite a bit. Territorial imperatives and all that. There were other empty seats further up the carriage, too, so why pick on me? Helpfully though (I was nicely brought up) I moved my big blue holdall and my handbag to make room for him. She wanted to get on with pushing her trolley up the aisle and she needed him out of the way.

I was soon to see why. He was drunk. Very.

As he eased himself into the seat next to me I was met by a waft of spirits. It was so sharp, so strong. It wasn't so much that he was smelling of drink in the ordinary way as exuding it like an essence. The darkest undernotes of alcohol. Shaken up in a sudden cocktail of acrid and bitter.

I don't want to imply he was a tramp, or scruffy. There was nothing down at heel about him at all. He was bearded and pale, with a black and white Arab scarf round his neck, though I noticed that only later as he told me his story. There was something distinctive about him. He'd stood out in that crowd at Crewe and I can't quite tell you why. Earring apart I mean. He was different. Even the way of his drunkenness was different. Again I can't explain, other than to say that he'd retained his dignity and a terrible kind of poignancy. His face wore a startled, incredulous mask.

To look at he seemed to be a living contradiction, part hippie, part squaddie. And his tipple was whisky. However well lubricated he already was, there was obviously room for more. Before the girl had trundled the trolley out of our compartment, he was up on his feet again, if uncertainly, coming back with two of those miniature bottles. (I could tell even from the rear, by the girl's whole demeanour and body language that she didn't want to serve him at all.) He drank straight from the bottle. As if it were pop. And his face wore a strange urgency. The rest of us were tame, ordinary. He possessed a dark knowledge it pained him not to share.

I hope he doesn't get too pally, I thought. I felt very stuck, pushed up against the window, half obliterated by my holdall and bag. I was a captive audience.

It was now I saw the nose stud; silver again to match that earring in his left ear. With a kind of diamond in the middle, very bright.

* * *

'You tell stories don't you?'

I was eight. I was about to be interrogated by Mrs Stannard and I was standing by the back gate with my pet jackdaw on my shoulder.

His name was Coco. I'd bought him for half a crown (a lot of money, that; several weeks pocket money) from a bigger boy in our school, Alan. He was always hanging round the castle, climbing up on the crumbly walls where the different pinks and dark reds of Aunty Betsy grew in close tufts. There, and on the top of the Watergate tower near the river, jackdaws would gather squabbling and clattering. Sometimes the boys went there with air guns. I didn't ask Alan how he'd got hold of Coco. It was best not to know.

Anyway there I was, the star of the show with this feathered conversation piece on my shoulder and here was the formidable lady herself with her curt question, her accusing air.

'You tell stories don't you?'

'Oh yes. I like telling stories,' I said.

Bizarre as it sounds it was only years later that I realised she was calling me a liar. She must have been disconcerted by my positive response but she didn't show it. Mrs Stannard was nothing if not cool. I'd taken it for granted she was talking quite literally about the stories I told in front of the class for Miss Roberts on Friday afternoons in Free Choice. A shy child most of the time, though not above showing off my tame jackdaw quite shamelessly, I would always burst into narrative life whenever the spirit moved and whenever there were people obliging enough to listen.

But what did Mrs Stannard mean by telling me I told lies?

There was no way I would ever find out, though the oddness and awkwardness of the encounter stayed with me. Could she have been told I was a liar by my grandmother, who only the week before had reprimanded me for saying there were hundreds of cats in the garden when there were only two?

But that was exaggeration. Surely a different matter altogether.

Anyway, telling stories isn't telling lies, is it?

So why did those frank German eyes so unsettle me all those years later?

★   ★   ★

I remember little of the journey in terms of looking out of the window. I was too conscious of the man sitting beside me, the whisky quietly disappearing. It was February, the light of rare clarity, the Wirral shore sharply visible.

By the time we'd reached Shotton the whisky was gone. I sensed the man's restlessness immediately, a seething sense of disturbance, a raw energy. Above all a sense of sadness and loss, a negative power.

'I've committed an indiscretion, haven't I?'

His voice was insistent.

Now I'm not one of those people who think it's unwise to enter into conversations with strangers on trains. I felt it would be unwise not to answer, in these circumstances anyway, and on some level I don't understand, I had no choice. I wanted, needed to respond to the man's real anguish. It was tangible.

'What do you mean?'

'Sitting alongside a lady when I'm drunk. I was minding my own business, watching my gear at the back. Didn't want to disturb anyone.'

'It's all right.'

'Is it? I wish it bloody well was. I've got an excuse though. For being drunk like this. I've been travelling for three days. From Kurdistan. Just now touched down at Birmingham and they're sending me to be assessed in this bleeding Welsh place, what's it called, Plas Eryri or something. I'll be seen by these shrinks there.'

I gulped. I'd never heard of Plas Eryri but I could tell him what the words meant.

'Plas Eryri means palace of the eagles.'

'Sounds weird. Have you ever heard of it? It's in Bangor.'

'No,' I said.

Just lowering his voice a fraction he continued. 'It's a post traumatic stress unit.' He looked at me. His eyes were dark brown, anxious. Wearied. I looked at him. The eye contact was prolonged, unnatural.

'If I told you what I've seen in the last few months, well, years, you wouldn't believe me. You'd never guess what I've been doing out there for a start.'

I didn't say anything, just gave him a vague sort of nod.

'I've been doing the kind of crazy job only a drunk like me would do. You've got to be drunk or crazy. Take your pick.'

I was trying not to stare at the brilliant nose stud. He wasn't particularly tall. His dark hair was receding. He had an aura about him. Darkness. Great courage. Sorrow. Then darkness again.

'Out there,' he said, 'You wouldn't believe. Death, destruction. Human life counts for nothing.' He now turned towards me and looked at me very hard.

'I'm not a mercenary.'

'No.' I said.

'Mind, I've had my share of fighting. Ten years in the British army. The Falklands. The Gulf. Northern Ireland. The lot. What've I been doing now? Working in a minefield, that's what. He laughed. The expression 'hollow laughter' is common enough, but believe me you never heard laughter as hollow as this. 'Out there with a load of stupid buggers who'd have your ... bum blown off as soon as look at you.' He'd meant to say 'balls' but quickly changed the word as a sop to my sensibilities. I was strangely touched.

'Making safe. That's what I've been doing. That's what they call it. Making safe.' He toyed with the two words as if suddenly aware of their meaning. 'Not that you can, and it's a bloody dangerous process even trying. Years from now there'll still be kids, farmers, going up with a bang. Legs missing. Hands missing. You can't make it safe. Safer maybe.'

Again his eyes probed mine. We were level with a sea wall. Beyond it the Dee estuary was grey wrinkled calm.

'What I've seen ... No one knows what's going on out there. Or cares. These shrinks who'll assess me. Where I'm being sent. What do they know about anything? They've taken away my photographs. Some fella from the F.O. Took the negatives too ...'

Then came the laughter again. Exhausted hopeless laughter.

★ ★ ★

When I got home I told Jim about my encounter with the man from Kurdistan.

'Was he a Kurd?' Jim asked. A reasonable enough question I suppose.

'No. He was English. A bit of a Midlands accent. He didn't seem to know what was happening except that he was being sent to this Plas Eryri. Have you heard of it?'

'No,' said Jim. 'Sounds to me like someone's being having you on.'

'I'm sure it was true,' I said. 'He'd been doing bomb disposal work. Working in a minefield. It had really got to him. He was in a terrible state.'

'A blind drunk doing bomb disposal work? Pull the other one.'

I stared at him. His face wore a wry, amused look. It's one I know well.

I didn't say any more.

★ ★ ★

Beep, beep beep, beep, sang the lorries.

The class had gone. All of them. Helga had been the last to leave. She'd written a piece about the embroidery class she'd been attending. As always I was impressed by her industry, her commitment.

I was also sure that beyond the literal truth she always provided there was the capacity for imaginative flights. She denied them though, as if she were afraid. Perhaps she was right to be cautious. Perhaps the dividing line between fact and fiction is not one to be blurred, distorted.

I thought of the man from Kurdistan. I thought about him a lot. Had he been simply spinning me a yarn? What was the nature of the difference between Jim and me in regard to our receptivity? I was inclined to believe people, give them the benefit of the doubt. Jim was an arch sceptic. Always. With him it was automatic. His attitude to life was quizzical, testing. Our marriage only worked because we'd both learned pretty early on to accept that we were never going to be soulmates. We gave ourselves plenty of space. We didn't expect too much.

I don't often dream. They say though, don't they, that we do in fact dream three or four separate dreams every night but for the most part we just don't remember them. Maybe. The night before I'd had a very strange dream indeed.

It started on a train. We were moving through a war torn landscape. There were burned out tanks. There were bodies. I wasn't afraid, though. Strangely. I felt detached, even relaxed, although I was witnessing horrors, the aftermath of terrible human carnage. Then I got up and calmly walked through to a kitchen, one that seemed slightly familiar but which I couldn't quite place. We weren't on a train anymore. The kitchen was cold and thin with a high ceiling. There were cacti on the windowsill, some very large. I looked at them closely. The more I looked the more bizarre they became. And in the middle of a pale grey green cactus like a bendy toy Mrs Stannard appeared, surrounded by sprouting scarlet flowers.

'*You tell stories don't you?*' she said.

'No I don't,' I said.

'I'm glad to hear it.' She smiled at me. 'And I don't want to hear any more about it. At all.'

'You won't,' I told her.

I was glad too. I felt a wave of great relief wash over me. Outside the window a girl of about eight or nine appeared. It was Helga, flaxen haired and fiercely plaited. She was offering me a bottle, a very large bottle of whisky.

I moved effortlessly through the glass of the window and sat with

Helga on a railway embankment. We were giggling happily, swigging at the bottle. Out of my pocket I took one silver earring, a filigree thing. I fixed it carefully in my ear and then reached for the silver nose stud with the central diamond.

Leonora Brito
Circle-Way West to Circle-Way East

The schools? They've broken up, he said. An those that haven't broken up are breakin up. Then he got on the bus.

I went back inside the shelter. Saw them through a hole in the glass, coming up the track that runs by the woods. They walked in single file, the four of them. Two of them young and one of them older — and the girl, straggling behind with a small TV set in her arms. Oh they stumped up the track alright, but they missed the orange. The bus. They were just a foot away from the shelter when it sailed straight past. And their faces turned, and watched it go.

Fuggin buses! One of them, I think it was the older man, who shouted. Fuggin buses!

I stayed inside the shelter and examined the time-table. Pocked and pitted. The glass. Burnt sienna here and there, and a smoky, melted yellow over all. Clever, the lighted cigarette butts held in the exact same place, I thought. The exact same place where I want to — look? So don't look. Look instead at the holes in my canvas shoes; neatly darned with dental floss.

This grey metal bus shelter is a beautiful thing though. Beautiful, with the criss-cross lines over the glass to make it vandal-proof. Some kind of reinforced plastic glass that makes the colours go all blurry. Cold, sunshiny afternoon like this, like standing in front of a stained-glass window. Latticed, with the blurry reds and blues, and an intensity of yellow that's — actually nothing to write home about when I do take a look. A brick-faced wall, of honey yellow.

Cool? I'll make you cool —

He was talking to the girl, the older man. Stockily built, in a tight-fitting crombie, of midnight blue. A red bristle of hair, and red-brown eyes, like aniseed balls. A fuckin slag, the boys said in his ears. A fuckin slag! His nostrils flared, like the twin engines of a jet, because he had a tan, a tinny sort of tan; with an oil slick of sweat on it, despite the cold.

A fuggin slag! he shouted. A fuggin slag, I knows you.

Yeah?

The boys were laughing. And the girl was laughing too. Jerking her head to look out for the bus and answering. White canvas jacket, cheap black skirt, bumpy pink-white legs, no tights, she looked out

for the bus and answered him, yeah? Dark haired, the girl, and elfin.
I saw the small TV set at her feet. Portable, old white plastic that
was yellowing. Only black and white, I noticed. Not colour.

How do I know? How do I know you're a slag? the older man said.
I knows. He took a couple of steps towards her, then stopped and
reeled on his feet. I knows you're a slag, he said and shouted. I knows
you're a slag, because you looks like one!

Orr yeah! Above the laughing boys she said, orr yeah! The
bluebells in the dark woods by the built-ups, the houses, remind me
of something faded — this morning I opened my wardrobe door
and saw a bunch of old clothes that seemed to have flowered in the
darkness, then faded. Like a bush of faded, lavender blues.

You would, he said. You would, if I offered you enough money
you would — because you're a slag!

Alright, she said. Yeah, alright, so I'm a slag! An a prostitute, she
said. An a drug addict, an a thief. Do it inna back of a car for fifteen
quid —

Let those lips touch my — ! he said and reeled. The boys held him
upright, and laughed. You think I'd let those lips go near my cock?
Me, Jimmy Carbis — you're trynna make me look a cunt, he said.
A cunt, and waved his crombied arm.

Come back! The girl had stepped out into the road. Don't walk
away from me, he said. Don't walk away — I'm Jimmy Carbis. I'm
not a violent man — I won't lay hands on you or nothin! But the
girl stayed where she was, stepping out into the middle of the road,
as if she was looking for the bus. Come back, the man staggered and
shouted. Come back! Or I smash you inna mouth!

The bus came then. The little orange circle and the girl jumped
on it. The boys heaved the crombie-coated man up onto the
platform and left him swaying in front of the driver. Quick as a flash,
the girl jumped off and ran back for her telly. She hugged it to her
laughing, as she and the boys flagged down the 'bluebird', as it drew
up behind.

You gett'n on mate?

Stepping further into the shelter, I shook my head and smiled, no
thanks. I'm waitin for the next one! Through a hole in the glass, I
see the bluebells in the dark woods, by the built-ups. I take out my
felt-tipped pen and scrawl across the time-table: This shelter is my
home now, please respect it.

Duncan Bush
The Snowy Owl

I thought I'd better make sure to call in at the farm and have a word
with bloody Daio first, just to square it with him. Alright, so it's
paying off his debt, or some of it. But no farmer likes the bank selling
the land out under him. Anyhow, I rang him first thing after nine,
told him there was a buyer, it was all fixed, put him in the picture
about everything. Said I'd call half tennish.

It was just gone ten when I got there. I'd put half a dozen pegs in
and a hammer last night, but of course, I didn't have wellingtons in
the car. Didn't think of it, with it being so dry lately. The yard was
a midden of trodden cowshit just by the gate there and I had to
tiptoe around it, scale my way in in my good shoes, holding on to
the post. He always has been a dirty farmer, Dai. You've only got
to look at the backsides of his animals to know that. But that's how
these people live. I don't suppose his own is much cleaner, most of
the week. His father was the same. That's one tradition they keep
in a family like that, from one generation to the next: the general air
of dirt and dereliction everywhere you look. Even that yard itself's
more like a scrapyard than a working farmyard, what with the
chickens nesting in the old Morris and that tractor out of the
nineteen bloody forties parked there in the nettles to rust away since
it packed up God knows when, in the exact same spot ever since
I've been coming here, changing quietly from one red to the other.
But then, slap outside the door, the Daihatsu 4 x 4. And the Massey
Ferguson under the haybarn, two years old when he bought it. Then
he wonders why he gets out of his depth. Why he can't repay the
bank. I've seen it time and again, with these wheelbarrow farmers,
increasing their loans every year for new machinery, when all they're
doing is running half a dozen Friesians and a couple of hundred
bloody ewes up on the mountain side. I suppose Dai uses that tractor
to drop a few hay bales off up there in winter. As to all those parts
lying in the long grass there, plough and disc harrow and the Lord
knows what, for the amount of use they are to him, which is the
amount of level soil he's got that's deep enough to bother turning
over, he'd be better off with a donkey and a wooden rig, like the
wogs out in Egypt and places still use.

The door to the house was open and that wall-eyed bitch of his came out and growled at me. I stared it out and it licked its chops and slunk back in. Hello, I called. I leaned in and rapped the door with my knuckles. There wasn't a knocker. Hello, I shouted. Dai!

I thought, if he's out in the fields I'll have to go and find him. I'd deliberately told him a later time, to avoid that. I don't know whether it's pure happenstance or what, but he has a knack of being over the back end of the farm when he knows you're coming.

I rapped the door again. I know his mother's deaf as an oak post. I could knock until the crack of doom if it's only her in there. For a second I wondered, is she still alive? But I think she must be. I haven't seen anything in the local obituaries. She must be well into her eighties now.

I shouted in the door again. Then I heard a noise over in the barn. I went down to the bottom step and shouted that way instead. The yard was another swamp of mud and cowshit, and I was debating whether to edge round the near side, past the old pallets and other junk, when Daio came out of the big barn door. His arms were full of sawn logs.

Hello Dai, I called across. I laughed. I'm bloody marooned here, I said. I've only got these shoes.

He came across the yard straight through it. Green wellingtons, I noticed. The gentleman farmer, every inch of him.

Mr Thomas, he said. He went past me. You coming in? he said. Or what?

He went straight in with the logs, plus all the muck on his boots, not even scraping them, let alone turning to slip the damn things off his heel against the edge of the step. It takes a little while to get adjusted to the light in Daio's house. I almost had to feel my way along the passage after him to the kitchen. He dropped the logs on the floor by the grate. Anyone else would have unpiled them or at least bent halfway and tipped them against the wall. Dai just opened his arms and dropped them. He kicked back one that rolled across the floor. Now I could hold my hand out to him. He showed me the oil on his palm instead. Been having a bit of trouble with the chainsaw, he said.

How's your mother? I said. I put my hand away in my bloody pocket.

She's alright, he said.

Good, I said. She's a remarkable woman for her age, I said.

You have to keep in with these people. A small firm like ours runs on local knowledge, goodwill. On people staying with the firm. That's the only way we can beat off these big outfits with offices nation-wide. He opened the doors of the woodburner with the tool and threw a couple of the logs inside.

I suppose she is, he said. She's had a hard life. He poked into the stove and shut the doors. It looked dead to me. What's he plan on doing with this field? he said. This, what's his name?

When Daio talks to you he's direct enough, so far as words go. You might even think rude at times. But while you're looking at him his eyelids keep shutting and fluttering. It's like a stammer. But he doesn't stammer. He just bats his eyes, and doesn't look at you.

Clay, I said. I knew Dai knew his name too, and who he bloody was. I don't know, I said. Anyway, I've got to meet him up there in ten minutes or so. Just to agree the access in that bottom corner. Get it pegged out properly. I thought I'd call in first. Just to keep you in the picture.

Oh aye, he said, as if it didn't matter to him either way. Which I suppose it didn't since the bank was now owner, executor and vendor anyway.

We haven't agreed a completion date yet, I said. But once we do I'll let you know. So you can, you know, get your stock off in time.

He took the kettle to the sink and started filling it. Duw, I thought. He's not going to offer me a cup of tea? Which I think would have been the first time anybody did, and I must have been inside this house a dozen times or more over the years, going back, oh, to when the old man was alive. He put the kettle on the stoveplate. Better make another bottle for my mother, he said. She's in bed.

Make a bottle, he said, like for a baby. Hot water bottle, he meant. Though it's the same thing when they get to that age, I imagine.

Oh? I said. She's not poorly, I hope?

She's alright, he said. They get like that. Some days she don't seem to feel like getting up. He gave me that fluttering look. Except, this time it fluttered at me instead of away. It was the first time he'd actually looked at me without me having already been looking somewhere else. I bloody feel like that myself some days, he said.

With anybody else, that would have been a joke. I had to take it as one, anyway. Not a lot else I could do with it.

Don't we all, I said. Don't we all. I took a glance at my watch.

Well, I said.

We both suddenly looked to the bright square of window over the sink, where this black and white cat had jumped up on the sill outside. It had a bird in its mouth, a sparrow or something. The stone wall was so thick, the aperture tapered in. The wood of the frame, you could see, was soft with rot.

He came out to the step. I thought he might want to come down the lane to the field with me, to see we put the pegs in right. I'd called in partly for that, to give him the chance to if he wanted to. I suppose he would have been within his rights, or that at least we could have paid him the honour of a pretence he was. But he never mentioned it. So neither did I.

What's all this about this mad cow disease? he said. This BST, is it?

BSE, I told him. BST's British Summer Time, Dai.

I think it was like with Clay's name. I know Dai's dull. But people get names wrong that way deliberately. Maybe it's superstition: as if misnaming a problem makes it go away. I see it happening a lot in my business. The vendor doesn't remember the buyer's name exactly right, or the other way round. And I think that there it's probably a case of pure and simple hatred. Hatred and grudge and resentment. Because whenever you get a price agreed it's a better price for one side than the other. That stands to reason.

If you ask me, these big breeders have brought it on themselves, I said. They've been feeding stock this high-protein junk to fatten them up quicker, chicken heads, offal. It's contrary to nature, I said. A cow's a ruminant. Not a bloody carnivore.

Aye aye, Dai said.

He wiped his mouth and I noticed there was a thin streak of blood on the back of his hand. Then I could see the bleeding around that couple of teeth in his bottom row. He still hadn't had that gum infection cleared up. Trench mouth, we used to call it. God Almighty, he'd had that when I saw him last, at the sales in Brecon market. May, that was. All it takes these days is a course of penicillin tablets. He looked at me looking at him, or stuttered his eyes at me at least, and I caught the whiff of his breath. Like garlic gone off, it was. I moved down to the bottom step.

Anyway, I said. If the price goes out of the market for beef, that's who you've got to blame. The big breeders. It's their greed. And now it's backfired on them.

Not that there was a lot of point in talking about big breeders to Dai. Fifty years old and living with his mother. I looked at my watch. Anyway, I said. I'd better drive back down and meet this man.

★   ★   ★

So we pegged it out at the corners, Clay and I. I could see he was holding the buckle of the tape well shy of the boundary fence to start with, and the same with every marker peg we put in afterwards. But you've got to have them at one end of the damn thing or the other, and I'd rather give them that foot at the start than have them this end reading off the measurements in yards. Anyway, it was no skin off my nose, or Dai Light's. I didn't mind him wangling a bit of extra width off that unfenced portion. I imagine the National Westminster bank can survive a loss like that. It's not as if it's ground worth killing for for a kick-off.

I don't know what he plans to do with these bits of land he owns now, a field here, a couple there, scattered across the bloody county. There doesn't seem to be any system in his buying. You'd say he was just buying poor to average land up cheap. It's not as if he even grazes a horse on any of them, as far as I know. Though I think he did, a few years back, when he bought that piece above Sennybridge through us. I think his daughter must have had a pony then, or his wife. Very smart woman, his wife.

That's exactly ninety feet, I said. (Nearer a hundred by now, I knew. And he did too.) I pounded the last peg in. That's it, I said.

He followed the end of the tape slithering across to me as I wound it up. We stood looking at the plot.

What are you thinking of running on this? I said.

He ran his hand back through his hair. A bit, you know, vague, like he was thinking about this for the first time. I don't know, he said. It's been grazed to the bone this year. I think old Dai wanted to get every blade of grass cropped off before it goes. I probably won't do anything with it till the spring, he said.

There's a bit of rush in it, I said. (A lot, I could have said.) I wouldn't let that get the upper hand.

No, he said, I might get a couple of Galloways in.

Galloways? I said.

They're what you want if you've got rush in the ground, bramble, he said. I've been reading about them. They've had a lot of success with them in certain parts of France.

Is that right? I said. Of course, a Welsh Black'll do the same job.

He laughed. Mr Thomas, he said. Or I think I can probably call you Colwyn by now, can't I?

By all means, I told him. The patronising bastard.

He gave me a sideways look. You a Welsh speaker, by the way? he said.

Yes, I said, I am.

Ah, he said. The language of heaven. Only a joke. What I was going to say, Colwyn, is, I can tell you're a patriot.

I didn't mean that, I started to say.

Don't forget to pick up your hammer, he said. And he walked off with this little smile on his face.

He annoyed me, actually. Upset me. All I meant to bloody tell him was, he can buy Welsh Black calves on the hoof in Brecon market without going to the length and cost of importing a breed from Scotland, not to say France. Then again, I don't like anyone joking about my country or my language. Particularly a cunt like him, who's as good as English anyway.

He was waiting for me at the fence. I turned away to look at the field again because my eyes still had that hurt look. Sometimes you wish you could tell clients what you really think of them.

I don't know, he said. I might just start some woodland in there. Native species. Sow it with wildflowers.

Wildflowers? I said. I laughed. Not much return on them.

No. Not a lot, he said. He gave me this sideways glance again and laughed. You don't have to do anything with land, he said. If you've got to make a living off it you're in trouble. Look at the farmers round here. But if you haven't, you can let it sit. It'll always be worth more in the end.

I didn't say anything. I've been in this business thirty years in this area. They buy it through me, or they sell it through me when it fails or someone gives up or just dies. I make my living out of people who think they're shrewder than me. It's not even that I don't mind letting them think it. It's probably essential that they do.

Anyway, when we'd packed up he invited me back to the house to wet my whistle. I looked at the time. I had to go over to Halfway to give a price on the old post office, which is coming on the market. Not a bad spot. But a bit close to the road.

Alright, I said, if it's just a quick one. Thanks. I'll follow you down in my car, shall I?

To be perfectly bloody honest, I didn't especially want to raise a glass with him. But it was on my way. And, aside from anything else, I thought it was a chance to see inside the house. Business is business.

And it's true enough, what I'd heard. He's got some good stuff in there. You know: not the ten-a-penny bought-in farmhouse look, authentic. There was this Victorian sideboard in the one room, mahogany, with ropework piers and bevelled mirrors and shelves and cornices and the Lord knows what. It was big enough to stand behind a hotel bar. I say Victorian, but it didn't look English to me. It might have been continental. Beautiful work in it. But of course, you'd have to have a room that size to put it in.

There was a lot of china stuff and knick-knacks and pictures and old tools, and so on, I don't know about things like that. It's not my interest. But it all looked worth a bit. I mean, there were no horse brasses and miner's lamps. It was all the real McCoy. I don't actually know whether it's him who's the collector, or his wife. We didn't see her. She must have been out, I thought.

Anyway, I didn't look at anything too close. I made a point of not noticing. Let alone complimenting him on anything. Normally I would. It's a courtesy that goes with the profession. And sometimes showing interest can be as good as getting a bid in early, because people remember when they want to sell. But some people don't seem to need a compliment off anyone except themselves, and they're getting enough of those already. Let me put it this way. He's always struck me as a man who likes himself well enough never to have to worry about being popular.

To be fair to him, that wasn't why he asked me back anyway. I think he's gone past showing his taste off to occasional visitors. He didn't make any effort to, you know, offhandedly draw my attention to something, the way people do. You'd be amazed how many men (I'm not just talking about women now, but men) are houseproud. Or proud of a single bloody article of furniture inside the house, even. I mean, they'll usher you through to some broken-backed commode or third-rate reproduction cabinet, and from the modest smirk across their face you'd swear for all the world it was a living shrine.

The only thing he did want to show me was those birds in cases, and it was me who brought that up. I asked him about the one on top of the bookcase. Just you know, for something to say. He said it was a Golden Plover.

It's not a bird I think I've ever seen, I said.

No, he said. I don't suppose it is. Then he looked at me suddenly. Come upstairs a minute, he said. I'll show you something else. You can bring your drink. Hang on. Let's top you up.

But I covered the glass with my hand. I don't like to drink red wine at that time of the morning, especially when I'm driving. I'd have thought he would have offered me a glass of beer or something, as it was such a warm day. Or at least offered me a choice of something, instead of coming in with two poured glasses. I expect he had an opened bottle. Frankly, I'd have preferred water. I followed him up the stairs.

This is my study, he said. My point of production. He did pause for a moment then, as if to give us time to, you know, admire it.

You've got a few books, I said. They were piled in the corners under the slope of the roof, like they were holding up the bloody ceiling.

This is just some of them, he said. Most of it's just twenty years' worth of review copies. Postal freebies.

He took me across to this big glass-fronted case. There you are, he said. I'll bet you the price of that field you just sold me that you've never seen one of these before either. Not in the wild.

Well, I said. It's some kind of owl.

He nodded, looking at it. He said a name in Latin.

So what's that in English? I said.

It's a Snowy Owl, he said. He said it as if it was Jesus's shaving mug, with the razor and brush still in it. Or was, he said. Believe it or not, this one was shot in Breconshire, in nineteen hundred and two.

Is that a fact?

That's a fact.

I went close up. It must have stood over a foot tall on the perch. It was gripping this fir branch. On the floor there were some fir cones floured with snow. It had big yellow eyes. The feathers were pure white, with a sooty-brown mark in them like ermine, but more like a barring. It had furred claws.

God knows what brought it here, he said. They're almost unheard of in Britain. Perhaps there was an exceptionally hard winter, and it just came further and further south.

Looks like a fine specimen, I said. Probably worth a bit of money now, is it, something like this?

Do you know where I got it? he said.

He didn't answer my question so I bloody ignored his. I looked at the bird and waited for him to have to tell me.

I got it out of Tŷ Mawr, he said, when old man Carew died.

Really, I said.

We'd got to know the family a bit, he said. I went to his funeral, actually. Not that we'd been here long. But I got on quite well with old Carew. He wasn't a bad old bastard, he said. Considering he came from a family of coal-owners and philanthropists.

I remember when he died, I said.

Anyway, his widow decided to sell up that big old house and move somewhere closer to their kids. So she sold off just about everything in the place.

I remembered that too. Clee, Tompkinson and Francis did the auction. But one of these snob firms in Mayfair handled the sale of the house.

Anyway, he said. I managed to get this. I got in before the dealers, so to speak. He shrugged. I gave the old lady a fair price for it. You know.

I'm sure you did, I thought. In counted, one-pound notes.

We looked at the bird. You could see it was a first-class specimen. You almost expected those cold yellow eyes to blink once at you, sleepily.

All the way from the Arctic Circle, he said. And some cowboy around here shoots it. A bird like that, he said. Rarer than a fucking angel. He drank off what was in his glass. It was his third. He looked at me. Some things come once in a human lifetime, he said. If they come at all.

I'd have said he was tipsy. You know, the way a drink or two at mid-morning can affect you because you're not used to it at that time. Not that I got the impression a drink was a complete novelty for him at any hour of day.

I looked at my watch. I said I'd better make a move. We went on down the stairs. He stopped suddenly in the hall and looked at me.

Colwyn, he said. My wife's left me. His voice broke on it.

Has she? I said. I didn't see what else I could say.

We stood there like an awkward couple or as if we might have been about to bloody kiss. Then he shook his head and looked embarrassed. Forget I mentioned that, he said. He led the way on out through the kitchen. I almost asked him about that big Welsh dresser, but I couldn't now. I'd have liked to know what he paid for it. Not that he would have told me: for all the talk he's got he's as close as the wallpaper around his rooms. Not that I suppose he had any intentions of selling it. But just, you know, out of interest. And circumstances change. People die or go bust, or marriages break up, and suddenly everything's put up for auction. In my business, you never know when they're going to phone you. You're the next call they make after the undertaker.

We got out to my car. Well, I said. Now it's up to your solicitors and the bank's to fix a date for completion.

Thanks, Mr Thomas, he said. Colwyn, I mean.

I'm sorry about your wife, I said.

Forget I told you that, he said. Will you?

Whatever you say, I said.

We shook hands and I got in. I was already going to be late at Halfway, I knew. I hadn't earned much that morning for the time and petrol; just the commission on a four thousand pound piece of ground.

I went out over the gravel. It sounded like pouring water. I wound down the window to let the heat out and the air in, and looked out, passing Clay's neat, striped lawns and flowerbeds, the gateposts of dressed quoins with the stone balls on them, and the double iron gates. I thought of old Dai up there in his bloody dark dirty infested farmhouse, hanging on somehow or other in the middle of all those sold fields like the last yellow tooth in his head.

Tony Conran
Gladioli*

Dug from staked redoubts
Dry gladioli
Corms on a tray,
Yellow and crimson lake,
Gleam like a battery
Of conkers in battle array.

But look, somehow old,
Ancient as elves,
Mushroom or lobsterpot.
Firm-fleshed and crinkled,
They keep to themselves
In our drawerful of drought.

It is April. Bare
And wistful as stones
They must go to the soil.
They have the cold air
Of autumn round them,
The shoot frozen in foil.

Not like daffodils
That in a trice
Would sprout, or snowdrop
Bulbs that seem to be still
Dreamers of green —
There's no key to this lock.

And yet, the reserve
Of elf veterans
Takes to the field —
Courage stronger, nerve
Keener, the long pikemen
March, slope arms, left wheel.

* Lifted after the first frost and planted again in Spring.

Bellis

Daisies walk the lawn
Like a factory floor
Keeping union rules
In the closed dawn,
Opening shop before
The boss comes in his Rolls.

The 'eye of the day,'
Llygad y dydd, but
That's not true of them —
Multiplicity they
Represent, the guts
Of the New Jerusalem.

Even the eye cocked
Up to the Daystar
Is manifold,
A chapel of frocks,
Never a singular
Bloom in the fold.

Each thin floret a flower
A factory lass
White as magnolia
In the Marxian power
Of a working class
Crowding towards day.

Asplenium (Wall Rue)

The pre-wall wall-rue
Crouches down a cliff
Of crumbling limestone,
A tribal rendezvous
For the wedges of leaf
Meticulous, dull-green,

A sparse populace
Of tiny ferns
Gypsy and swart
Travelling the rock face
With a few dogs, hens,
A bullock cart.

On every wall for miles
Their brothers thrive
With cushioned moss
In unmistakable style,
Dapper-tufted, alive
To the scam and loss.

They court obscurity
Like secret immigrants.
Walls made their fortune.
Brickies obligingly
Bedded them out, instant
Civilization, room.

But yet, the pre-wall
Avatars, the tribe
Before mortar was thought of —
Alone, as if all
The thousand and one nights
Of the Diaspora —

All the rude histories
In the letters home —
Didn't count at all,
Were of a different species
To these, who plod wild stone
To the next waterhole.

Tony Curtis
California Burning

The pool ripples red
under a black and grey sky.

This is a nightmare at mid-day,
one long exhalation as the country burns.

White walls are graffitied with smoke;
the End announced by each burning bush.

The pool furniture re-arranges itself
into a group of reclining figures.

The windows are stained glass,
then crack. The tapestried drapes

unravel, their patterns unpicked into gold threads.
The suite smells of burned animals.

Les Beigneurs enter the river.
Portraits weep, then picasso themselves.

The one abandoned car cooks
then demolishes the garage.

The roof shuffles its pack
and slaps its hand down noisily on the table.

Some say a careless camper;
some say a freak

with the sort of eyes that flame
behind dark glasses.

Along the block, one white house
stands untouched behind its bank of ice-plants:

the heat squeezes their water
and quenches itself elsewhere.

This is how the dreams burn,
the lies we compose play themselves out.

All the ease that money can buy
crinkles like old bank-notes in a furnace.

Down the Road

After months of standing empty
next door's been bought —
builders vans parked outside for weeks,
white plastic windows are going up;
the metal frames they've taken out
are stacked inside the stone wall like broken spectacles.
The stucco's painted white.

Miss John left last year after a second break-in,
kids probably, drugs probably, the young copper said.
Right through the house and into her bedroom
for thirty quid.

We've visited her twice in Orchard House
where, 'It's nice enough,
not like a hospital'.

In the early hours, in the afternoons,
false alarms trigger from houses
up and down the road.
Electrical faults, too much rain,
too much sun, cowboy fitters.

Approaching a restless fifty,
for the first time in years
we talk of moving.

The traffic's become a flood.
Crisp bags, drinks cans, cigarette packs
litter the hedge and lawn from schoolboys
and college apprentices training to be cowboys.
Signs and niggles.

As I towel myself in the bathroom
a Tesco bag caught high
in what was Miss John's sycamore
flickers and waves in the sky.
Through the frosted glass it could be the moon
or a white flag.

John Davies
Gold

Whatever the place is called,
'isolation' it's pronounced.
The dirt road
is a ghost hunt by a snake.

When gold showed up,
people grabbed it and ran.
Things keep running,
all down.
Though the sign says *Pop. 12*,
the old man thinking
hard with both hands
makes it nine. Or ten.
He recalls meat so tough
his fork stuck in the gravy,
'a loyal two-woman man'
with an eye for the frame house
recently abandoned.
One day it could be his.

Patched by movers-on,
the place looks stunned.
Back there under a cloth
and tin box marked *Cutlery*
is a table
somebody did not return to.
One day it will be yours.

But just off the road
set in tangled water:
stones which, held up at arm's length
were skylights
fresh from being undervalued.

So what if none were nuggets,
flecks in the urgent flow?
Dirt roads assay their worth.

The News from Tokyo

We stayed awhile
with my brother in New York.
He was caretaking for Mrs Minami,
Tokyo millionairess, who'd left
her favourite colour.
Florid porcelain, bureaux,
winged chairs, angels everywhere,
were pink in the style of Louis
the Predictable.
Our voices echoed and rococoed.

In Tokyo, money had dried up —
faxes arrived, stuttering,
the phone a question mark.
Gareth plugged holes
but rain kept nosing in.
Fake covings flaked

on walls an unhealthy rouge,
on Mrs Minami's aim to 'Wrap
a Pink Ribbon Around the World'.

A veldt of carpeting kept feet
off the ground. Around homespun talk,
silks rustled that weren't ours.
Sweat worked when air conditioning
would not.

In three acres, as cicadas
zipped and unzipped trees,
boulders or slabs of old testament
kept growing.
And stone showed through inside,
pink rinsing out, the place
groping back to basics
as we'd have to also
if we'd remembered what they were.

A Short History of the North Wales Coast

All right, agreed, just a low shelf
piled with hills. Still, it was itself —

incomprehensible come rain or war,
life folded, you'd say, in a bottom drawer —

till the railway's sudden drum
thundered 'customers'.

Bingo. Both sides across stunned ground
snuffled like truffle hounds.

Came a blue surge of matelots,
quaintesques, glee parties, pierrots,

and the Palace saw a real African kraal
stretch to gondolas on a canal.

St David? Slept in magic groves a span?
Would have sold out, *Dave the Fasting Man.*

Here anyway in an early photo,
like an advert a house on show

foreshadows what's all spick and spent.
It is the ghost of crisis present:

on her lawn like a Welcome mat,
a lady addresses a caged bird. Just that.

With the parrot though, so many
ears unlearned so much from opportunity

that tongues licked brandnew speech.
And all changed. Like that. It's teaching

time at Bagillt where our lady misrule
has started-up the Parrot School.

Christine Evans
Safeways

The yawn of early afternoon's the time you'll see
women just too young or too far to be grannies
slow trolleys that they steer deliberate as prams
between the aisles of crisps in Family Packs
and ice cream in a score of flavours, pause
as if in meditation of Mr Men yoghurt, even hanging back
from the shrillness of the check-out scrum

to watch mothers tethered by their infants
and feel again the tug, the never-sleeping
sense of extension. They know all about
the weariness, the play and sting
of mutual friction: their eyes are soft,
but wryness twists their lips. As long grass
shoots in spring and thickens round

a holed bucket or last year's machinery
left to rust by the farmyard wall, their kids
have grown through them, moved on.
Good, once, to keep the blades at bay
and make a lee, part of them can't help hungering
(keep that flowered apron, Nan's recipe for fudge)
for function. Relic status. Rediscovery.

Inbetween

Jangle and smash of breaking glass

make a wound I fall through
to the steps inbetween
kitchen and washhouse
where the bottles went flying
when the clot in her brain
tripped the hurrying blood
and she crashed

the gauze wings of her dress
webbed limp around her
healfingers clenched
on the thorns of white roses
she breezed in with, like a story.

I kicked at the milk crate
nine summer weeks later
and threw myself down
snuffling sour milk and mildew
letting slate's cold hold me.

In the other room, she was
different, a grandmother
I was taken to visit
a stubby four-year-old with a solemn fringe
her grey gaze wandered over.
Her feet stuck up like islands
or like tree-stumps in the snow.
Everything grew pale about her —
long fingers playing on the air
or stroking, stroking
the sullen tabby that I schemed
enticing upstairs to my bed.
They fed her white stuff too,
not-milk, its smell of rusty nails
dug up in the flowerbeds. Once
I had to hold the feeding cup
she sucked at blurrily, like a sick kitten.

She dried and shrivelled to
a dry cocoon, a husk
I could see belonged in earth.
In those weeks the language left
in the hills above Cilfaesty
forty years behind
caught up. Jerked-out
words that slowly started
to make sense, became what I could salvage
and now give breath to daily:
'gwely', 'cariad', 'cysgu'.

Catherine Fisher
On the Tower, Hereford

Climbing the stairs, the tight turns
are an idea you can never grasp,
twisting into darkness. Legs ache,
the wall is cold; echoes shuffle
from someone far ahead. Always,
there's someone up ahead.

Climbing the lantern; edging round
a crack in stone. Under my toes
people hum in the nave's spaces.
Angels hang here, dusty.
This is pride, this is folly.
If no-one wants to pass me I'll be safe.

Climbing the ladders. They lean
on vaults, a cage of timbers.
Names and dates cut them deep.
Crawl here, the roof over you,
weight of wood on your shoulders.
The door tiny, like a tomb's.

Through it. The leads, high, vibrating
with bells, thrum of flagpoles,
the sky blown away to Powys.
Heart throbbing with words
to take down without spilling.
And no-one here; no-one ever here.

Secrets

The piece of chalk lies on the step, and every time
he passes he picks it up and draws, outlines,

nothing she can recognize. Spirals mostly, like those
cupmarks out of archaeology, the mazes

that mock us all from megaliths, simple
with withheld significance. The lump

of chalk is stolen from some downland; it powders
smoothly on the pavement in his fingers

and she's reminded of that story in the scriptures
where Christ wrote on the floor for his accusers.

They pour from him, the curving lines, as if they were
    the sun,
or the hot afternoon turning to the dark, or the spin

of his emotions winding on themselves, until he throws
it down and looks at her and says 'I wish I knew'.

Cromlech

Ridged like the sea's back,
like the moon's profile pitted, cratered;
cupmarked with mosses, bone-grey;
creature turned fossil, craving drink.

Crouched before it, crawling in it, arms full of dark,
I feel its weight poised, grinding the uprights,
crushing antler, rammed chalk, down to the powdered
bone. I asked not to feel this and haven't,

till now, palms in the soft mud;
ravenously swallowed. Eaten whole.
Like them I bring my dead here cleaned to memory,
without speech, fleshless, seen only in sleep.

This could be any time; the may spilling
white in the grass; rain down fingers,
down the spine of the stones; taken at their word
someone crouching here, between claws.

Paul Henry
The Rainbow Workshop

for Tony Goble

Soft hammering of brushes.

The secret formula waits
in phials, jam-jars, pots ...

Night pitches the moon's top *C*
over *The Brothel of the Fallen Angel*

Red.

Flexing his wings, he hums
Mendelssohn's *Hear My Prayer*
measures out the paint-potion.

Time is already against him.

Orange.

The first diaphanous cloud
slips across the skylight.

Yellow.

The choir boy's voice in his head
breaks as a lone drop cracks
an oily pane in the alley below.

Prospecting for dreams, he knows
there is no gold in rainbows.

Green.

And you are watching in monochrome —
his palette a labourer's
barnacled mixing board.

A pigeon dressed as a dove
shelters under an ancient eave
and turns into a lorikeet
as the rain starts to applaud.

He perseveres, blindly,
with teaspoons, candles, glass,
wood ... the detritus
of wrecked centuries.
The blueprint comes back to him.

Blue.

He begins to smile, deluded.

His fingers trace a scree
of dislodged vocabulary.

A cross uproots itself in the gale.

He believes in the colour of Braille.

Dawn draws its deadline
under the furthest cockerel.

Indigo.

He nudges open the frame
and stands back.

It soars over the town,
arching the grey, dazzling slate
and a few stray souls.

Violet.

A plane takes a knife to it,

far away, far away ...

Douglas Houston
Retirement

Their modest gardens balance in the sun,
Bright emblems of the rectitude and peace
The pension plans have offered on release
From work and lives that meant its will was done.
Uncertain narratives still left to run,
The plots are incomplete until they cease,
Absorbed into the nature they must police
With poison now the slug wars have begun.
Since father died of ten years such routine,
Well armed with jigsaws when the winters came,
He visits in a dream and seems depressed,
Makes failing efforts to explain he's been
Unable to come home, says work's to blame,
Is looking forward to a well-earned rest.

Conditions

Dragging a bad tooth up the mountain,
Light gets through the mist exhausted,
Stains the snow grey, blackens rock.
A raised lip ducts in freezing air
To cool the answer to 'what's wrong?',
Chiefly ageing, pain, decay,
While the one hailstone in history
That will enter my ear
The instant I lower my hood
Is somewhere out there and closing.
Dragging a bad tooth over the summit,
Past the locked refuge, its steel shutters
Bolted down and crusty with ice,
And the lakes below are sailing on
Through windows torn in brown cloud,
Their levels pure as a lucid theory
That survives the mountain's vast upheaval.
Dragging a bad tooth down to the sunlight,
Doped on success and endorphins,
A spray of hail drifts in on the breeze
Each white pellet with the momentary grace
Of hope entertained in good time.

Mike Jenkins
Time is Dribbling Away

I read on-a bus shelter
wishin I coulda wrote
summin tha clever.
Idin in my ood
in-a misty rain,
waitin fer them girls
oo pass this way,
a- perms o' ferns

coverin the valley
like-a damp autumn
couldn go away.
Up yer I'm left be'ind:
it's ard t' see-a black,
the grass 'ey planted
slike 'n astral turf.

Where 'ey goin 'en
them two crackin girls
oo won' even turn
theyr gorgeous eads
t' where I'm unched
in my concrete coat?
The streams 're dribblin
like gob on-a chin
o' some ol nutter.
In New Tredegar
a-clock's stuck on twelve,
coz time's water
mockin as it goes
t' places I'll never get t'.

I stare at theyr orsey bums:
like a whip my mate
ee rises so quick.
I spit on-a pavement
opin 'ey'll look back
at-a throttle o' my throat.
My mate ee's solid as a brick,
won' keep still like a ferret
want's t' climb, t' get out,
while all's I do is sit.

Still Learning After All These Years

Windowless above the track to Cardiff and beyond —
the Scala: once dry as a minister's celebrations
now wet as the spit of his preaching.
Picture-house, flicks, I once saw a movie here
where I couldn't make out one word.

On my gravestone: He Finally Conquered Mutations.
A skin called Knobbler, a bevy of alkies
one looking for someone to attack.
The juke-box plays The Clash,
it's an English Civil War but I'm not sure
who's fighting, coloured balls are smashed
and Man. Utd are on the box again.

Through to the spacious room with its single green,
with its longing for Cabaret acts telling the one
about the Scotsman, English man and ... Welsh
and English soon co-habit the air uneasily,
Saesneg hiding in pockets, Cymraeg like fingers
of phrases making marks in the dust.

Each table's a level: I won't reach the bridge
never mind cross it. Our tutor's got a case
the size of an altar. Some clutch dictionaries
like Bibles. I scribble, scribble, scribble:
the Future I'll forget tomorrow.

Tonight it's Calan Gaeaf, nostalgia damp
as beer-mats, but still we try to make sense
of thrown pebbles in harvest fires
which blacken hands by morning, to be stored
like words through winter. It matters so much more
than the yearly burning of Guto Ffowc.

Stephen Knight
The Music of the Spheres

Sing a song of crow's feet,
of spectacles and Steradent

      of blistered paint, of brittle leaves
      while rattling a light bulb

            harmonise with headless dolls
            and broken spines of paperbacks

or, rallentando, jingle change
in pockets that are losing it

      sing a song of cobwebbed socks,
      of laughter-lines and liver spots

            join in with faded furniture,
            praise dirt around the light-switch

serenade the stars with dust,
with flowers stooping from a vase

      or croon a phrase that echoes in
      the hole where Richmond ice rink was

            sing a song of black snow
            and hymn the peeling heels of shoes

for everything that wears away
hum, cantillate, chant, whistle, trill

      you know the tune.

Near Wild Heaven

Waking to silence underground

among torn copies of *The Sun*
I see one other passenger —

his Walkman, his darkened raincoat

dripping, his brittle *A-Z* ...
While rows of armrests glow

trains moan in other tunnels.

Time passes, drop by drop, and I
watch London fall to pieces

thinking I know the song.

The Rain

I dream of murderers
and burials and rain
the noise of rain
rain spattering the bed
drenched blankets
clinging to my legs:
in rooms my daughter
emigrated from
I search for dust;
I touch the tops of doors
the skirting boards;
the dents in every carpet
fill with rain;
and though the walls
are painted white
the pattern shows —
peering, I make out

lines of leaping fish
twisting in the air.
  I stay all night
I cannot wake
until, at five o'clock,
first light arrives
washing me ashore.
While the kettle boils
I read the postcards
on my fridge door
one more time.

Gwyneth Lewis
The Love of Furniture

I

I think today I'll wear my dresser,
the oak one, with my grandmother's

china, the set her father bought for her
in Aberystwyth. I fancy lustrewear

and cake plates. Royal Albert's the future
of punk. Not everyone has hardwood to wear,

a set of brass-handled drawers.
But I have inheritance. So there.

II

I dreamt about us last night, my dear.
You were a wardrobe. Behind your doors

on hangers my best desires —
cocktail dresses sequined with fear,

velvet trousers, tartan skirts,
wet-look raincoats, satin shirts

all tinged with the smell of camphor,
a whiff of lavender. You were

capacious, held far more
than I'd ever dared to want before.

You were kind and so I picked out
a soft, well tailored, shimmering suit

that sat just so as I made my way
out through the door and into the day.

III

The sofa bride is a pair of lips
for two to sit on. Upholstered hips

are made for the distance, padded, sewn
into satin or taffeta, buttoned down firm

for one owner. No diamond on a cushion he,
but as for her ... the right *chaise* to be

longue on for ever, for she'll take the strain
of his weight for the honour of changing her name

and to show him, much later, a cabriole limb
in exchange for minute of moving with him.

IV

In battle all men shall remember
never to endanger the Admiral's furniture

on pain of death. It is essential
that the commander's gate-legged table

be stowed in the hold. It is worth far more
than the chap who made her. In times of war

chattels come first. If the hold is full
and the orlop deck cluttered with terrible

bodies, then, seamen, be sure to launch a boat
and fill it with hautboy and with sideboard

for the enemy has agreed not to fire
on his fixtures and fittings for — to be fair —

which of you can say that you've shown
such loyalty to a man of renown

or such service as Lord Nelson's china and silver?
Lord Nelson's desk? Lord Nelson's easy chair?

V

There have been tales of great self-sacrifice
on the part of furniture. Take that chest of drawers

in the Kobe earthquake. When the building fell
it flung itself down the tumbling stairwell

across its mistress who, pregnant, lay trapped
in the rubble for days. Its rosewood back

took the strain of girders, of vertical floors
by marquetry's artifice, while the usual doors

buckled and closed. But its sturdiness
became her pelvis, allowed her to press

down on her daughter, helped her give birth
out of pulverized concrete and earth.

Macramé mother, whose dovetailed joints
gave life to another! though the effort meant

total collapse once the rescuers came
with shawls and shovels to ruin the frame

that had saved the baby. Now, once a year
on a certain date a woman and daughter

visit the grave on a building site
where scrap wood was burnt. Lest they forget.

Leslie Norris
Peaches

In his life he has made seven gardens, two
from the untilled meadow, some in good heart
after the spades of other men. One, unkempt
inside its formal Georgian walls, he brought
to perfect order out of wilderness, its geometric
beds to flower, renewed its lawn, cut back
its gnarled espaliers and clipped their trimmed limbs
to the limestone. He remembers the rough bark
of those old varieties, pears mostly, and how
he hit the supporting nails into the mortar.

This is the first time he has grown a peach tree.
It is the third year of the small tree's bearing,
and already his black dog has cleared the lowest
bough of its green fruit, nibbled the flesh,
left a scatter of kernels about the grass. No matter,
there's plenty. He has posted a stout cross
beneath the branches, else a heavy harvest of peaches

pulls the whole bush down. Watching the early blossom
has been his pleasure, the frail brevity of blossom
blown in cold weather, then the incipient fruit.

He does not walk in the garden until evening,
the days too hot for his uncovered head. When shadows
spread from under the trees, he stands there,
near a dusty lilac, surprised by hot gusts
out of the desert. His roses are abundant now.
He has let them grow and mingle, throwing their trails
over and through the massed green of other shrubs.
Alba and gallica roses, damask roses, centifolia roses,
an old moss rose, a bed of hardy rugosa. Refreshed
by roses, he cherishes the garden air, his head filled

with generations of perfume. Far in his life,
he nods to the spent iris, remembering how in water
his yellow flags stood high, how as a child he took
in his father's garden bright vegetables from the soil,
and how in the autumn hedge blackberries glowed.
It is his way of life to desert his gardens.
The neighbour's evening lamps light up the peaches.
Fruit is ripening, orchards everywhere ripen.
He throws a fallen peach to his black dog.
The animals were not expelled from Eden.

His Father, Singing

My father sang for himself,
out of sadness and poverty;
perhaps from happiness,
but I'm not sure of that.

He sang in the garden,
quietly, a quiet voice
near his wallflowers
which of all plants

he loved most, calling them
gillyflowers, a name
learned from his mother.
His songs came from a time

before my time, his boy's
life among musical brothers,
keeping pigeons, red and blue
checkers, had a racing cycle

with bamboo wheels. More often
he sang the songs he'd learned,
still a boy, up to his knees
in French mud, those dying songs.

He sang for us once only,
our mother away from the house,
the lamp lit, and I reading,
seven years old, already bookish,

at the scrubbed table.
My brother cried from his crib
in the small bedroom, teething,
a peremptory squall, then a long

wail. My father lifted from
the sheets his peevish child,
red-faced, feverish, carried
him down in a wool shawl

and in the kitchen, holding
the child close, began to sing.
Quietly, of course, and swaying
rhythmically from foot to foot,

he rocked the sobbing boy.
I saw my brother's head,
his puckered face, fall
on my father's chest. His crying

died away, and I
read on. It was my father's
singing brought my head up.
His little wordless lullabies

had gone, and what he sang
above his baby's sleep
was never meant
for any infant's comfort.

He stood in the bleak kitchen,
the stern, young man, my father.
For the first time raised
his voice, in pain and anger

sang. I did not know his song
nor why he sang it. But stood
in fright, knowing it important,
and someone should be listening.

Richard Poole
Black Bag

In a time of disillusions
and failed exorcisms,
he took from the black bag
the tongue of a dictator
and thrust it into the flames.

There it spat out syllables
of blood, blackening,
crackling in the fire's tongues
that leapt like a lioness,
clawing down air.

Out of the bag came
the hands of an assassin,
the genitals of a rapist,
the conscience of a minister,
the ears of a judge.

Still the bag was full.

Words overflowed it —
words divorced now
from mouths that had uttered them,
pens that had written them,
presses that had printed them.

Words, in his dreams,
came drifting like snow:
braziers ate it
but it clothed every contour
in shame and silence,

melted on dry tongues,
infecting the blood of citizens
like a plague ...
                    Waking, he shivered
from the black ice of the news,
shouldered his bag and went on.

Rain

There were so many killed a single cemetery
couldn't contain them — not even a cemetery
as big as the world. Unsurprising then
that it should rain the names of the dead.
He cupped his hands and held them out
and a shower of Jews splashed into them:
glittering, the names caught the broken panes
of the world, flashing them up into his eyes.

He threw the water down, but his hands were still wet.
Puddles were at his feet, raindrops gleamed on his toecaps,
culled from the monuments of a thousand civil wars.
In the rain-haze of the street visibility had shrunk, but
a man was coming towards him, hat coat trousers shoes all
black black black. He carried a red and yellow umbrella.
Off this the names of the dead gaily bounced,
as from a trampoline. 'Dreadful weather. Ridiculous.
Was it you who prayed for rain? Why? There wasn't even
    a drought.'
The man bared his teeth. Was he smiling, or angry?
A bureaucrat perhaps dispatched by HM Government.
Bosnians poured from the rim of his umbrella.
The first man turned away. 'It's nothing to do with me.'
The unpronounceable names of Aztecs
plastered his hair to his skull, ran down his face into his
    eyes,
trickling like a punishment down the back of his neck.
His trenchcoat was no help. Would he ever be dry again?
He shook himself like a dog, scattering names in all
    directions.
Rain like this went through your clothes,
got under your skin and into your bloodstream,
could thumb an easy lift direct to the brain.
He looked hopefully up to the sky. It was bucketing
    Chechens.
Best to go with the flow. He opened his mouth
and stuck his tongue out, possessed by an urge
to know the flavour of the rain. Drops pattered steadily
    down,
a clear cold liquid shed by neutral heavens.
The names had no taste
but his mouth was filling up. In the future when he spoke,
it would be with a different voice.

Two Riley Grace Poems

Blood

Round and round goes the blood, so simply.
Under the skin and through the heavy heart.

You grin limply, a disempowered Merlin.
You have no chart for this outlandish ground.

I touch the blood in the bed. This is the dead time.
Absurd rhymes go tumbling through my head.

Blue

I'm blue tonight, blue — like empty sky.
There's only one colour to colour me by.

As if an iron bluebell rang in my head.
As if my tongue was cast in blue lead.

I knew he wouldn't come. I knew his knock
would never interdict the formal clock.

I've drunk a bottle of curaçao straight —
and blue midnight's come, my dreamy date.

I've kissed the mirror's icy eyes.
Glassy. Unseeing. Vomited up his lies.

The phone is off the hook. I'll crawl to bed
and dream of sunrise. Cold. And blue. And dead.

Sheenagh Pugh
Polgar Dreaming

'Walk properly, there's no need to be draped round each other making people sick.'

The boy and girl drew apart, self-consciously, and Mr Morris watched them turn the corner of the building.

'What is it with that class lately?'

Miss Ames sighed. 'I don't know, they seem to have started a fashion for falling in love. Perhaps it's just the time of year.'

'Randy little swine. I'll take the lads on cross-country, next time I have them for games. That'll cool 'em down.'

The boy, safely out of sight, put his arm around the girl again and muttered: 'Sad old git'.

There did seem to be a certain current of electricity in that particular form-room. Innocent remarks were charged with unintended meaning; bodies which had been shapeless bundles in uniform suddenly set pulses racing. It was as if everyone were ready and waiting, needing only the slightest encouragement to trigger them off. Rhys Roberts, husky-voiced after a heavy cold, caused little moans of delight whenever he spoke in class, and Louise Rabaiotti, who happened to have sleepy, heavy-lidded eyes, moved in a cloud of boys like midges. She had objected at first, but now found them handy for carrying things.

Gareth watched from the sidelines, cultivating a pose of amused detachment. It was what he did with all fashions; it was expected of him. His classmate Alan, calling round to borrow a textbook, was surprised to see, on the wall of Gareth's bedroom, what looked like a concession to the current fad: a poster-size photograph of a girl's face.

'Hey, I don't know *her*. What class is she in?'

'She isn't. That's not some girl, it's Judit Polgar.'

'Judith who?'

'Polgar. Hungarian. Chess player.'

'Oh, is that the one you went to Hastings to see in that tournament thingy?'

'When she tied with Bareev to win the Premier, yes.'

'Oh ... Nice looker, though. I like all the hair. Is it really as blonde as that?'

'Like a lion.'

'Yeah, cool. I'd sooner have the real thing, though.'

Gareth did not pursue the subject. He hadn't minded Alan noticing the photo, though he wouldn't have been so obvious as to draw his attention to it. And he liked to hear her admired. But he knew no-one at school would see her in the way he did, and he certainly had no intention of explaining why he preferred her to the real thing.

Mr Price, the history master with whom he played chess sometimes, knew he'd been to Hastings for the tournament. Gareth did not mention that he'd gone more to see her, but he did drop her name into the conversation, casually, when Price asked if he'd met any of the players.

'Two of the Polgars. I got Judit's autograph and I saw the middle one, Zsofia — she wasn't in the Premier, just the Challengers.'

'Ah, the Hungarian trinity. They put me in mind of a set of moon-goddesses.'

'Eh?'

'Go and look it up. Try Graves' Greek Myths.' Mr Price never gave an answer if he could send you to a book instead.

Mr Morris carried out his threat of taking the boys on a cross-country, and was chagrined to notice how they shook off their tiredness and put on an impressive spurt when passing the court where the girls were playing netball. Only Gareth, sauntering along at the back, made a point of not changing pace. Illogically enough, that annoyed the games master still more.

Later, in the corridor, Morris saw a group of boys and girls on the other side of a glass door. One of the lads was doing what he suspected was an imitation of him, haranguing the rugby team before a match. He smiled ruefully at the caricature of his own enthusiasm, but it was Gareth's huge yawn in response which infuriated him. He burst through the door, shouting.

'It's all a joke to you, isn't it, the team, the —'

He had let the heavy door swing back without wondering if anyone might be coming behind. Miss Ames was, in fact, with her arms full of books. Gareth reached behind him and caught the door, easily, before it could hit her. She thanked him warmly, accepted his offer to carry the books and spared a freezing glance for Mr Morris in passing. Gareth smiled. He knew he would come in for some

classroom humour about fancying Miss Ames, but any day when
he got the better of a games master was a good one.

That night he dreamed of Zsusza.

She was the eldest of the chess-playing sisters, the only one he'd
never seen, and perhaps because of that the clearest in his mind.
Zsusza. Such a soft, dense mouthful of consonants, and that round
u sound, like someone trying to talk with his face buried in a girl's
hair. Moon; full moon. Older sister. Strange, he resented his own
older sister, with her infuriating air of experience and superior
knowledge. But after their games of dream-chess, Zsusza, with
infinite patience, would analyse his play and tell him what was wrong
with it; and though still he never won, he didn't mind.

Sometimes they didn't play chess, but just walked and talked, and
again he didn't mind her knowing more than he did. It was relaxing,
being taught; like leaning back in a warm bath. She was engaged
now, he'd heard, to some Peruvian player. In the dream, she told
her fiancé that she would have to bring her younger brother along
to live with them after they were married; she was firm about that.

Zsusza had been the first of the sisters to enter his dreams, maybe
about a year ago. He dreamed of them all fairly often now, but for
a long time it had been only her.

Next morning in class, it was Robbo who made the expected witty
remark:

'You goin' to ask Amesy out, eh, Gar?' It came with a gust of
unmalicious laughter. Robbo was handy in a scrum: built like an ox
and with about as much thinking power.

'Yeah, that's right.' Gareth grinned and went along with it; the
boy's unsubtle attempts to sound macho; the girls' sarcasm ('She
wouldn't give you the time of day anyhow') until Mr Price's
entrance put a stop to it. As the class settled, and he found his place
in his book, Gareth became aware of, rather than noticed, Sarah.
She never did anything to get noticed: didn't play an instrument, or
sing, or get into trouble, or shine at anything. She wasn't bad
looking, but five minutes after you'd seen her, you would be at a
loss to say what colour her hair was or what she had on. He'd only
noticed her now because of something she hadn't done; she hadn't
joined in the joking about him and Miss Ames. Maybe she just had
no sense of humour. Or a better one than Robbo.

Mr Price, who happened to be their form master, held a notice between finger and thumb with distaste.

'You may possibly be aware that the last day of term approaches.' He waited for the cheers to die down. 'I am instructed to announce to you that on the last afternoon, instead of devoting ourselves to knowledge, we are to repair to the hall for something called a disco. Dressed appropriately, which I presume means inappropriately for any civilised place.'

He was hamming up the High Court judge act, which he enjoyed. The class, or most of it, was wild with delight, the history lesson forgotten. Gareth cursed inwardly, as averse to the idea as Mr Price could have been. He knew nobody would be allowed to sit quietly in a corner with a book: joining in and enjoying oneself would be expected, and Gareth wasn't at all sure how his own habitual act would play in such circumstances. There was a difference between sitting on the sidelines because you wanted to, and doing it because you had no choice. Alan, Rhys and the rest were all bantering with the girls, getting half-promises to dance; even Robbo was cajoling the glamorous Louise; the great mutt was too dim to notice the mockery in her warm, slow voice, but Gareth heard it and shivered: no way would he risk that ...

The mood he was in, he was not altogether surprised to dream of Zsofia.

He had seen her at Hastings, doing moderately in the minor tournament while Judit was winning the major. He had not thought to ask for her autograph: she was just Zsofia. The middle one; neither one thing nor another; her name, even, a pale echo of Zsusza's rich mouthful. The least successful of the three, and the one who was rumoured to be still in it only because the others were, and she didn't know what else to do. Half-moon, half-talent. A lot more than his, sure, yet he felt sorry for her in Hastings, and somehow in his dreams as well. When they played dream-chess she beat him in an embarrassed sort of way, as if it were a con she might be found out in: sometimes he managed a draw, which he'd have thought heresy with either of her sisters. Sometimes it struck him that, of the three, she was much the most like him, and his pity for her was tinged with alarm.

The last day of term was approaching far too quickly for his liking, and the class was pairing off. It was becoming obvious that, to retain any credit, you had to be able to say you were going to this disco

with someone. People he'd known all his life as individuals suddenly
went around being half a couple. Alan was hanging out with a girl
who had always got on Gareth's nerves; she had a high-pitched
giggle and her dull blonde hair smelled of cigarette smoke. Gareth
told himself he wouldn't ask *that* out for anything. But if he could
have been sure she'd accept, he probably would have. Suddenly
every time he looked at a girl, he imagined her saying 'No'.

There were ways you could be different, and ways you couldn't.
He could never get this across to his mother, when she complained
of yet another ruined rucksack.

'It's the way you sling them over your shoulder on one strap, it
puts all the weight on that side so of course the strap goes. You
should use both straps, I'm always telling you that.'

And he was explaining that he couldn't, that nobody did, but she
couldn't see it.

'It doesn't generally bother you, being different.' She had no sense
of priorities, no understanding that whereas despising rugby, or
affecting to fancy Miss Ames, might pass for interesting eccentricity,
someone who slung a rucksack on both straps would just be written
off as plain sad. Staying out of fashion in the right way was as delicate
and tricky as staying in.

Gareth was getting scared. His constant dreams of Zsofia, with
her sad eyes and competent, unspectacular game, made matters
worse. He began to see that he had always wanted to be not just
different, but special; he had always nursed this comforting assump-
tion that there was something about him, some talent, which would
eventually lift him out of the ruck. Standing apart as he did, trusting
no-one's judgement but his own, he had never had to test this out.
He was dreading the thought of, in effect, inviting someone else's
judgement on him.

He could see himself alone, and no pose sufficing to explain why.
Christ, even Robbo was fixed up, having settled for something less
than Louise. (*She* was still unattached, but then she could afford to
be; you could get away with it if you were known to be able to pick
and choose.)

He concentrated on the image of Judit at Hastings, trying to make
her return to his dreams. The swift walk of someone who knew
where she was going; the way she looked so at ease signing her
autograph, knowing her fame was something earned and natural;

knowing she was special. He remembered how the young British grandmaster had called out to her once in the corridor: 'Hiya, killer!' And the serious face in its golden mane had broken into a smile. But when she played Bareev, her eyes were pale, expressionless, and Gareth could see where the nickname came from.

He had long since looked up Mr Price's trinity of moon goddesses, and smiled at the aptness of it. But it fitted Judit the best. He could so easily see her as a young moon, a cold, pale curve of silver. There was that metallic hardness and brightness about her; it took his breath away. He was never sure, looking at her poster, whether he fancied her, or wanted to *be* like her, to have that certainty.

But all the time, he was getting less certain, and more apprehensive. One night, the turmoil in his head invaded his dream world, where he found himself playing a simultaneous quick-fire against all three of them. He had to keep switching his mind from one board to the next; to concentrate on it and blank out the others. From Zsusza's elegant, inscrutable pattern, which he was sure hid a trap he hadn't spotted yet, to Zsofia's stubborn defence, which would take hours to break down, if he ever did. And Judit, advancing so surely, her attack simple and unanswerable, not least because he didn't want her to lose. He woke exhausted in the morning, feeling he had not slept at all.

It was that morning, though, that he began to see a possible solution to his problem. He opened a door, with exaggerated courtesy, for a group of girls, and amid the crossfire of jokes he heard again the one voice that was silent. Sarah. She smiled at him, but didn't speak. He watched her as she moved off down the corridor, already a little apart from the noisy group. He didn't know much about her; like him, she kept herself to herself. Maybe the shy front hid something interesting, or maybe, as he half suspected, she was just a fairly dull little character who kept quiet because she had nothing much to say.

What interested him more was her opinion of him. Over the next couple of days he made occasions to speak to her casually, when they were unobserved. She seemed surprised, reasonably enough, since he'd never paid her any attention before, but not unwelcoming. Rather the opposite, in fact. Though her conversation never kindled, her face did, at his slightest word, with an eager gratitude which he found disconcerting. She looked, he thought impatiently, like a spaniel about to be taken for a walk. And then he felt guilty, and resolved to be nice to her at the disco — for he was certain now that she would go with him if he asked her.

With this load off his mind, he put off the actual asking to the last minute and relaxed into something far more like his old self. The anti-fashion stance, the hostility to anything that looked like enthusiasm, the wry comments from the sidelines which his friends had missed over the past weeks, were all back in force. He was not the class clown; he had never allowed that to happen; but a jester, maybe; someone licensed to poke fun at what others took seriously.

Mr Morris had been inoculated against that kind of humour soon after birth: it was inevitable they would clash again. It happened on the athletics field this time. The boys were high-jumping; when it came to Gareth's turn, he did the run-up but veered aside at the bar.

This was a common enough thing for any boy to do, if he felt he'd got the run-up wrong, and there was no real occasion for the games master to take notice of it. Perhaps because it was Gareth, or because some of the girls were nearby, or just because Morris was in a bad mood, he did.

'You! Why didn't you jump?' He had a carrying voice; not only the boys all around but the girls further off paused and waited for developments. Gareth saw Sarah among them, looking worried, and Louise, eyeing Morris with a contempt it was well he had his back to, and Alan's girl preoccupied with a chipped fingernail.

'Come on, I'm waiting! You've always got an answer to everything, I'm sure you had some good reason?'

'Cowardice, sir. I'm terrified of getting hurt.'

Morris clenched his fists with frustration; he would have liked to use them. He knew there was no way he could make anything of it; the words had not been said impertinently. It was a matter-of-fact statement, made without any intent of humour — or any feeling of shame. The damn boy was immune to the mockery he could have heaped on any of the others. He turned on the onlookers instead.

'There's nothing to laugh about. Get on with something!' He strode over to the long-jump pit, as if he had just noticed something that needed seeing to.

'Nice one. Very classy.'

Gareth had been watching Morris go. He turned at the voice, and found himself looking straight into Louise's eyes. They were big and very dark, with a keen glint of fun in them. Seeing her so close, Robbo cleared the bar with a massive leap and looked hopefully at her.

'Very good,' she said encouragingly, 'keep that up and you'll be a games teacher one day.' Her voice, close to Gareth's ear, was so musical and rich, it made his spine tingle. He said something trivial, his mouth dry. Her long black hair gleamed blue in the sun. She smiled at him.

Gareth's head was buzzing. It had never occurred to him that the image of an outsider might attract the fashionable, nor that he would stand any chance with the likes of Louise. But he did; it was unmistakable. Closer to her face than he had ever been before, he saw that its loveliness was not a matter of perfect planes and curves, but of light and animation. He felt his mind kindled from hers; though they had never exchanged more than a few words before, they fell easily into talk.

Even as he spoke to her, he was aware, with a sick feeling, of the figure hovering in the background, not putting itself forward. He had not actually asked Sarah to go to the disco with him, but he had surely given her reason to think he would. If he did, it would only enhance his maverick image to turn down the girl everyone fancied for one nobody had noticed ... And he would stop feeling as if he were about to hurt something small and harmless.

Louise laughed, with a sound like a river on stones, and he made an inarticulate noise in his throat and his whole being went out to her, as if to something he had been starved for.

It was Zsofia, that night, who came into his dream. She played a Caro-Kann defence to his king's pawn opening; apologetically, in an unconvinced sort of way. But there was no heart in his own play either, and it was basically a drawn position until the endgame, which he lost slowly, with infinite care, so she should notice nothing.

Anne Szumigalski
Jesus

A child sees Jesus coming towards her through the glass of
the nursery door. When his reflection fades, she turns around,
and there he is standing right behind her. She knows him by
his beard, by his pierced hands, by his bare feet, cold on the
linoleum. He bends down to kiss her, and she notices that his
crossed halo stays there on the wall above him empty, waiting
for his head to fit back in.

She's pleased with the visitation of course, but she'd much
rather he'd sent an angel with long feathered wings to lift her
up and fly with her over the tops of trees, over oceans full of
rocky islands with seabirds nesting on them.

Her mother has warned her that he is simply a man, with all
the things a man has: bristly chin, hairy knees, bony feet, this
and that. Sooner or later, her mother has said, he will come
for you and take you on a long journey.

The child glances outside, and sure enough there is a very old
donkey with downtrodden hooves tethered in the garden.
The scruffy-looking thing is chewing on some lilies in the
perennial border. Spotted orange petals and black tipped
stamens are scattered about on the grass.

Jesus has his arm around her now and is urging her through
the door and down the path towards the back gate. Panic, like
a long-necked bird, is opening and closing its beak in her
throat. Nothing comes out, not even the crumbly hiss of a
murrh.

She looks back at the house, at the nursery door still standing
a little open. 'I should go back and shut it,' she says to the
man who is squeezing her shoulder with large possessive
fingers. He doesn't answer, but points with his other hand
towards the road, where she sees her mother getting into her
small yellow car. She has on her big straw hat, the one she

wears for picnics. Her father is already sitting in the passenger seat. He has taken off his glasses and is breathing on them, first one side and then the other. Just as the car moves off, he holds them up to the light and begins polishing the lenses with his large, white pocket handkerchief.

French and English (a game)

The French are quite right about their language. Even in these polluted times, it retains a certain purity. Even when it is translated into English, its stringent nuances shine through, as the incorruptible corpse of a saint shines through a shroud.

Or, perhaps, it is a tower standing in the middle of a field, a tower strongly and delicately built of white marble. A good many men, and lately some women, dressed in splendid uniforms, guard the tower night and day.

English, on the other hand, is the feral field itself. Once cultivated, it is now overgrown with weeds and wildflowers. Very likely, this is because the farm keeps changing hands, and every husbandman has his own idea how things should be run. What one sees as neglected land, another views as summer-fallow. It is at the point now when nettles are growing in the hollows, and one part of it has been used, on and off, as a garbage dump. There is even a dead donkey in one corner. The poor thing has been lying there for some time. Flies are buzzing round its head; birds are pecking at its eyes. Poor old English donkey.

Time passes, and the flesh of the donkey becomes maggots, becomes grassroots, becomes raven's wings. Tell me, which language would you rather speak — stone tower language or dead donkey language? Don't forget the flies.

Halinka

It is right, they say, to bury a stillborn child with a mirror on the pillow beside her. That way, at the resurrection, when she opens her eyes for the first time, she will see her face and recognize herself.

But that's not for you, little daughter, little flaccid creature. For you, there never was such a thing as a face. There were hands and fingers, curled feet with curled toes. There was a heart in your chest, red and whole as a candy, and a white iris growing in the place of your understanding.

The Cranes

The interior sounds the body makes — how do they escape to the outside air, to ears other than our own, though we try to close every orifice? We make sure the eyes are lidded, the ears plugged, the mouth and other sphincters puckered tight. That leaves just the nostrils and they, of course, are continually busy, taking in and pushing out small gulps of air.

And haven't we all heard of the woman whose infant wailed in the womb? She got up to go to him, but could not find him, though she searched the whole house. At last, she remembered he was within her, kicking and crying from the other side of her flesh.

As for me, too late have I resolved to keep myself to myself. Though my fluids may leak out, I'll take nothing more in. The result of this must surely be an inner desert, as arid and gritty as the great sand hills, where in summer cranes walk and call. In autumn, they gather in the dunes and fly south to another desert, even hotter and drier than this one. And somehow, when they return, there is always one left behind, alone as I am, crying out against the solitary fate of females. But why should I need other companions, with this child lying in the crook of my arm, his closed and veiny eyelids, his mouth sealed with a soft white smegma.

How pale he is, barely breathing. There is only just time to awaken him before his sleep slips into an internal state. Before the sound of his cry is lost to this world, and to me who invited him into it.

As So Many Do

The day starts bright as a songbird. Later, it turns grey and begins to drip. Wings of clouds mantle the town where melancholy grass is beginning to turn yellow at the roots.

It was a day like this I had a fit of grief on the bus so that my tears wriggled down my face like rain on the window glass. The man behind me tapped me on the shoulder, offered a blue cotton handkerchief. The woman beside me dug in a damp paper bag and handed me one of those sugared dough-nuts that are so gritty and hard to swallow.

Afterwards, I noticed I had accepted the young man's arm. I leaned on him as we walked homeward, his shoulder wet with my sorrow. Or was it simply the drizzle dampening every surface?

When we reached the house I wouldn't let him go, and so he sat down beside me on the bed limply smoking. After a while, we both dozed off, bundled and sinless as I thought then.

I awoke to find he had taken off with several of Harry's things, which were still lying about the house — a pair of pigskin gloves, two antiquarian books, and a black silk umbrella.

Now he might have needed the brolly, but what could he possibly want with rare books, a man I didn't even know the name of. I made enquiries. He wasn't a local boy.

On dark afternoons like this, I open the curtains wide and sit obviously reading under the soft light of the lamp. Surely the rain will return that stranger to me, he of the cool consoling hand, he of the light fingers.

Bigos

Speculation comes easily to the man who can't tell the difference between this and that reality. His habit is to accept or reject each day, as though it was nothing more than a scrap of roasted lamb, offered at arm's length, on the point of a knife.

Often he dreams of severed limbs, but is never quite sure whose arms and thighs these once were. He has decided it doesn't matter. He likes them like that, unattached, flung far from what lies at the centre. Far from this head, whose mouth speaks endlessly, as though it might be a sin to leave a breath's pause on the tape.

It's only when he's gone, the one distance, the one direction possible, that we can bring ourselves to play the whole thing back. And then, of course, he seems to speak to us out of another time. But is there more than one?

That was always his question, and now that he's out there, it's natural we should think of him carefully gathering up the dust of his bones, for every atom of this white grit must be fitted together before he can begin on the flesh, his answer.

His wife dries her tears on a napkin of leaves, and lies with his brother under the open sky, calculating the propinquities of genes. For her there is no extension or bending of the light. Her desire is to get on with this life. But first she must find, in the depths of heaven, his one clear abiding star.

So perfect is her longing, that she has forgotten the iron pot, left balanced over the campfire. By now the hunter's stew has burned to the metal.

All night the lovers scrape and scour. Will they never be able to divide one substance from another?

Polynomal

The nun/midwife tells a certain young mother that god has truly blessed her, for she has been chosen to bear quintuplets. What an honour!

But the woman weeps, picturing the litter of infants lying within each other's curves, every which way within her womb.

'Foolish girl,' the nun says, 'dry your tears. You are not carrying all these babes for yourself. One is for you, the rest are for us sisters, the holy ones. They will be ours and ours alone, until the time comes to give them back to the Pleroma.'

The mother dreams of hiding her children in places where the light cannot touch them. At first in the drawers of her bureau, later in the thick woods behind the house. In her dream, she covers them over with dark veils, sometimes of cloth, sometimes of matted leaves.

'Nothing can be hidden from the Immutable', explains the careful midwife, as she swaddles the babies in white bandages. One at a time the nuns carry them out to the car. 'Here, this one is yours,' and Sister Superior turns at the door and tosses the last child onto his mother's lap. 'If I were you,' she says quite kindly, 'I would call his name Jesus.'

Caryl Ward
Trip

Well, it's too late to change my mind now. I'm in and I won't be able to get out for another five hours. Five hours, another country, another life. My handbag is on the floor between my feet, and an overweight man in a dark suit is sitting down beside me. He has thick-rimmed glasses, thick dark-graying hair, thick lips and a thick briefcase on his lap. He introduces himself, some German name, which I forget as soon as he tells me, and his voice is thick too, guttural, as if he's got a gob of phlegm stuck in his throat. And it's the last thing that I want, to be sitting next to Mr Thick for the next five hours.

The stewardess is doing the life-jacket routine, and as usual no-one seems to be taking any notice. She looks like the woman that they have on the TV news for the deaf and dumb, standing up front gesticulating, mouthing away. The plane is taxi-ing towards the runway, and I look out over the wing, see him waving, arms outstretched, like a solitary cross on the outdoor observation platform. I wave back, although I know that he can't see me.

The engines are screaming, and I feel the elation that I always feel leaving the ground. I don't understand why some people fear flying. To me it's the utmost feeling of security. To be enclosed by strong metal, tens of thousands of feet in the air, knowing that I'm going to be watered and fed, knowing that nothing short of the ultimate disaster can hurt me. And if that should happen, it'll be quick, and I'll be out of it all then anyway.

The no-smoking lights go off. Mr Thick lights up, and I take my cigarettes out of the bag between my feet. He smiles at me, offers me a light, and we're fellow conspirators, lepers, smokers. He opens up the conversation with a story about how two weeks ago he couldn't get a smoking seat, and as the flight was eight hours, by the time they landed he was suffering from nicotine withdrawal symptoms so bad that he couldn't walk straight. I agree with him that it's hell if you're hooked.

The stewardess comes around with the drinks trolley. I wasn't going to have a drink, just try to get some sleep, but Mr Thick is offering to buy me one and I ask for vodka and tonic.

Mr Thick hands over some dollars, and then tells me that he never carries cash nowadays except when he's on a plane or public transport. He got mugged a hundred yards from his hotel in New York city three years ago, they got away with eight hundred dollars, his credit cards and his Rolex watch, so now he wears a cheap plastic one.

I ask Mr Thick what business he's in, and he tells me concrete. He's got his own concrete firm and his main competitors are Costains. I'm impressed. I've heard of Costains concrete — worldwide and all that. Mr Thick he might be — but he's also Mr Concrete.

As the vodka goes down, and he orders us another and tells me about his home and his wife and two teenage sons in Germany, he becomes less Mr Thick and more Mr Concrete. He becomes more solid than thick, like concrete itself. I begin to enjoy his company.

His wife is headmistress of a school in Bonn, and his sons, he mentions their names but I forget them as soon as he tells me, are sixteen and fourteen. The younger is a keen sportsman and the elder is more academic. I tell him that my two are the same, and we laugh at how different as chalk and cheese our children can be.

Mr Concrete doesn't see much of his family. He's round and about the world on his business. He's going to a conference in a hotel near Heathrow for a couple of hours, and then he's booked on a plane to the Middle East, where he'll be for the next week, and from there it's Paris, then Luxembourg, and than back to Bonn and the family for a few days. He seems happy with his lot, and I wonder whether or not Mrs Concrete is happy, with her credit-card carrying husband forever on a plane or in a conference.

The vodkas go down pretty fast the way Mr Concrete drinks, and I keep pace with him. Eventually he produces an inflatable neck pillow from his briefcase. I've thought of buying one for myself, but it's always seemed a luxury. Mr Concrete insists that I use it, and for the first time in my life I manage to sleep rather than doze on a plane. And I dream. I dream of a woman without a head. The headless woman is carrying a large key, and she is wandering around a neighbourhood trying her key in various doors, but none of them will open.

I wake with a jolt, as if I've been snoring and my own noise has woken me. Mr Concrete is awake and smoking, and the stewardess is pushing the trolley up the aisle. She hands over the plastic trays, the usual hard bread roll, butter, jam, and square bowl of fruit salad.

Mr Concrete, bless his thick lips, orders two bottles of champagne and turns a miserable meal into a feast. We toast each other, clink glasses, and say 'Have a nice day'. Mr Concrete orders another two bottles, and we laugh and say 'Have a *very* nice day'. There's still two fingers in my glass when we begin circling before coming in to land, and I want to make these two fingers of champagne last forever. I want to stay in the air, where I'm secure and happy, with Mr Concrete sitting next to me talking and smiling.

But the stewardess is collecting the glasses, and the no-smoking signs and fasten your seatbelt signs are on, and we're coming down. I grip the arms of my seat and brace myself for the bump — but of course, there isn't one. I'd feel better if there was one, something to jolt me back into reality, to tell me I'm on land again, back here again. But the landing is smooth and we're taxi-ing and the wheels come to a stop.

And Mr Concrete is gathering up his briefcase, and smiling and shaking my hand and saying it's been nice meeting me and ... But Mr Concrete, you can't just go like this. Don't leave me please Mr Concrete. How would you like some company along with you? — like *me*. Take me with you please. Yes *you* Mr Concrete. I'm talking to *you*. You with your thick glasses and your thick hair and your thick lips and your thick voice and your thick briefcase and your thick wallet, and you can even stick your thick dick into me between flights and conferences.

'Yes, it's been a pleasure meeting you too. Have a good trip to the Middle East. And yes, well, you never know, it's a small world isn't it.' Is it?

Heathrow is disorientating at 7:45 in the morning when you're slightly pissed. It wouldn't be so bad if I was pissed enough not to care, but I'm in that state of heightened awareness induced by a bit too much, and yet not quite enough, alcohol.

But ha ha, you bastards, you can't ask me any questions here. I've got a big black British one, with gold lettering.

The bags are coming through on the conveyor belt. I'm standing with the others, trolley at the ready. We're all watching intently, and I remember my father when I was a little girl running his forefinger around the palm of my hand.

> Round and round the garden
> Like a teddy bear

One step, two step
Grab your bag from there

But I don't want to grab my bag. I want to leave it going round and
round. I watch it going past me, when all around me people are
claiming theirs. And then I see the other one, my two well-travelled,
scratched, Antler suitcases, no distinguishing marks, but I'd recog-
nise them amongst thousands anywhere. And I don't want to know
them. I wonder what happens to unclaimed baggage, and I picture
a huge pit, a burial ground of suitcases piled one on top of each
other, as I retrieve them and push the sum total of my life through
the green, GO channel, and I've arrived.

Hilary Llewellyn-Williams
Under The Lake

I
The Glass Ballroom

Whitacker Wright, clever
dealer and wheeler
at the turn of the century

in his gentleman's retreat
indulged a passion for secrets

for holes and passages
and mysterious entrances
to something underneath

and for woodcut fantasy:
the door in the holly tree
with mildew steps down
to an underground river

where a boat glimmered
floating between the worlds —

and the tunnel under the lake
to a ballroom of curved
glass, swallowed
in utter darkness of water

where the tipsy couples danced
warm in that airless place
by torchlight, silk to skin

as fish gaped sepia cold
lips to the thick streaked panes
drawn by a flickering
luminosity in the deep

a glowing dome
below them, a hollow boom
of voices muffled in folds

and rippling scales
as the cellos shuddered like under

water thunder, and the shut
door to the tunnel roared
and wallowed.

II
The Tunnel

This was the lake you could walk under.
There was the dogwood lake, where a man drowned;
there was the fishing lake, where my father waited;
and there was the big lake, with its secret
swallowed in it. It had a mouth:
it had a stomach of glass, and a black gullet.

On summer afternoons it gathered light,
spread it between the trees. It lay
face to the sky, its skirts bobbing,
lily leaves and reeds in its finger margins,
snagged in its hem. Dragonflies stroked its skin.

I knew that smooth complexion was a mask,
the Queen who gazed in her mirror —
underneath, shadows rucked
and wrinkled into a frown.

The packed unbreathable dark went down
down, netted with weeds, with the bodies
of fish nudging blunt and cold.

I knew its sucking power. It dragged me
as I slept. The gulf of bad dreams widened

and I lost footing, and I toppled in.

Now, I listened and stood at the open door
to the tunnel. It swung

inwards, and the echoes hurried up
from the black pit, to greet us.
The lake's dark body odour: stone's

cold sweat, the outbreath from a tomb;
a fishy taint led to the sunken womb
the inner chamber. Cunt of the Lake Mother.
I wouldn't go down there. I stood and listened

by the entrance as their feet boomed,
as their voices groaned and bellowed
from the bowels of the lake. I cried
for them until their heads appeared
across the water, mother, father, brother

on the viewing platform. They called
and waved to me, strangers, ghosts
from the other side, blurred and dim.
When they returned, they told me I'd been good —
but their touch was pondweed; they smelt
bad, like things dragged up from the mud.

III

The Viewing Platform

Over the warm stone
balustrade of this island
a child leans brown arms

face down to the depths
where terror slips
and opens a thousand mouths.
She is cast adrift

as under her the great dome
creaks with the weight of the lake
and the tunnel drips
between her and the shore.

She dreams that the tunnel door
        is locked

and water climbs the slope
from the glass chamber.
When she wakes she can't remember
drowning: just the fear.
A statue rises here, in the light
of evening, over the water:

the figure of Neptune lifts
his triple spear, with his fish
foamed round him, scowling

broad gilled, heavy lipped;
and merfolk, conch blowing
green from the choking weeds
who rise at his wish

his trident forked like the moon
held ready, motionless:
a steadying presence, as real
as her parents, and more

powerful. Who say it's turned
cold, we must go soon.

IV
The Curse

Under the lake, the drowned common:
the dug bracken, the levelled
tumps. What was scooped
and shovelled up by the workmen?

What did their spades disturb?

And was that statue bought
to keep the terror down
to stop the dark from rising?

Chaos caught in the guise
of guard, and gamekeeper —
no wonder he died so hard
no wonder the tunnel bellowed.

This park was our backyard
enclosed in its landscape:

three lakes, acres of trees,
swans churning the still
silver as they rose
in commotion, his mansion

on the hill — now gone beneath
a bramble tumulus —
something sleeping in the damp stables

and in the boathouses
each a water temple
lapping the shallows, a chill:

his initials a linked sigil
                 W W

whose spirit flew in the night
the voice of Whitacker Wright
in the chimney, dark twin
to Santa Claus, riding the storm.

The curse not laid by him:

under the lake, something older
stirring the thick green water

as Neptune closes his fist
awaits an implosion of glass

and fish swimming through
the dome; a bursting in
of the god at last.

Bagful

In your dream, you reach into my bag
to find it stuffed with hair.
Coils, hanks, skeins of black hair

nudge at your hand, a soft shock
like touching a furred animal in there —
but worse, this is loose, this is chaos

tangling your fingers, the damp filaments
that cling like algae. As you draw
your hand back, there is more, more:

nets, webs of hair, accumulation
of years, the brush-cloggings,
strands you find by the sink, the plug-pickings,

the hoover-spindle windings, the moult
on a towel, the broom-knots
twined into bristles, the pillow threads:

bunched-up, gathered, stored.
To think that so much has fallen from my head!
I could weave rugs from it, stuff mattresses,

mix it with clay and daub a whole house;
knit sweaters from it till my fingers bled,
hoard wigs of it against baldness.

You scoop some out, and shake it to the floor,
hoping someone will clear it up.
I will not; this is hardly my fault.

I have saved all my combings,
plucked them from the carpet, from the air.
If you must open my bag, that's your affair.

Drawing Down The Moon

First, clear a space for it.
The moon needs room to breathe,
to swell and shrink.
And don't just think of the white disc,
but the light around it.

Remove all rocks and stumps,
nettles and cabbages. Be
ruthless; this snare must be smooth
as a coin, and fine
as the skin of your eye.

Next, take a rope, and cast
your circle. May everything
in the ring attract moonshine.
Then hammer wooden pegs
around the shape, pulled hard

against the wind, which would carry
your garden, moon and all
away, if it could. Remove
your coat, and get digging.
Right down to the subsoil,

two foot deep in the middle,
shelving towards one end. Use
a level; if the ground tilts
your prize will spill. Heap the spoil
high to the south, for shelter.

Strew sand for a bed
and tread it firm. Ignore
your neighbours' sidelong glances
as you unroll stout polythene
to keep the precious rays

from running out.
Stretch it tight across the hole,
weigh it down with stones
and feed in liquid
to the brim. Stand back

in admiration. Wait
until nightfall. Say
the spell; and behold the moon
in your garden, swimming up
through nets of water.

Notes on Contributors

Dannie Abse was born in Cardiff and divides his time between Ogmore-by-Sea and London. His most recent collection of poetry is *On the Evening Road* (Hutchinson).

John Barnie hails from Abergavenny and is the editor of *Planet*. His most recent publications are *The Confirmation* and *The City* (Gomer). The stories published here are from a work in progress called *The Wine Bird*.

Glenda Beagan lives in Clwyd. She has published one collection of short stories, *The Medlar Tree* (Seren).

Leonora Brito comes from Cardiff and has recently published a collection of stories, *Dat's Love*, from Seren.

Duncan Bush lives in the Swansea Valley and Luxembourg. He has published one novel, *Glass Shot* (Secker and Warburg), and three collections of poetry. His most recent collection, *Masks*, was Welsh Book of the Year, 1995.

Tony Conran has recently published *All Hallows: A Symphony in Three Movements* (Gomer). He is the translator of *The Penguin Book of Welsh Verse*, now available from Seren as *Welsh Verse*.

Tony Curtis is Professor of Poetry at the University of Glamorgan. His *War Voices*, a collection of his poetry about war, was published by Seren in 1995.

John Davies comes from the Afan Valley. He teaches in Prestatyn, where he is Head of English. His most recent collection is *Flight Patterns* (Seren).

Christine Evans teaches at Coleg Meirion Dwyfor, in Gwynedd. Her most recent collection is *Island of Dark Horses* (Seren).

Catherine Fisher lives in Newport. Her most recent book of poetry is *The Unexplored Ocean*. She is also an award-winning writer of children's fiction.

Paul Henry lives in Newport. He has published one collection of poetry, *Time Pieces*. A new collection, *Captive Audience,* is due out from Seren in 1996

Douglas Houston lives near Aberystwyth and has published two collections of poetry, the most recent being *The Hunters in the Snow* (Bloodaxe).

Mike Jenkins is a teacher in Merthyr Tudful. His most recent books are *Graffiti Narratives* (Planet) and *This House, My Ghetto* (Seren).

Stephen Knight is from Swansea. He works as a theatre director in London. *Flowering Limbs,* his first collection, is published by Bloodaxe.

Gwyneth Lewis is a producer with BBC Wales. She has published poetry in both English and Welsh. Her first collection of poems in English is *Parables and Faxes* (Bloodaxe).

Leslie Norris's long awaited *Collected Poems* and *Collected Stories* will be published by Seren in February 1996.

Richard Poole is the editor of *Poetry Wales* and teaches at Coleg Harlech. His most recent collection is *Autobiographies and Explorations* (Headland).

Sheenagh Pugh lives in Cardiff. An award-winning poet and accomplished translator, she has published seven volumes of poetry. Her contribution here is one of her first short stories to be published.

Anne Szumigalski was born in London, lived for some time in north Wales, and emigrated to Canada in 1952. Her poetry has twice been nominated for the Governor General's Award, Canada's leading literary honour. All the work that appears here is taken from *Rapture of the Deep* (Coteau).

Caryl Ward was born, and lives, near Pencoed, Mid Glamorgan. She is an MA student on the University of Glamorgan's writing course.

Hilary Llewellyn-Williams lives in Cwm Gwendraeth. Her most recent collection of poetry is *Book of Shadows* (Seren).

Selected titles from Seren:

Anglo-Welsh Poetry	ed. Raymond Garlick & Roland Mathias		£6.95 pbk
Welsh Verse	ed. Tony Conran		£6.95 pbk
Abse, Dannie	*Intermittent Journals*		£6.95 pbk
	Three Plays		£6.95 hbk
Glenda Beagan	*The Medlar Tree*	fiction	£6.95 pbk
Leonora Brito	*Dat's Love*	fiction	£5.95 pbk
Duncan Bush	*The Genre of Silence*	fiction	£4.95 pbk
	Masks	poetry	£5.95 pbk
Tony Conran	*Blodeuwedd*	poetry	£3.95 pbk
Tony Curtis	*The Last Candles*	poetry	£4.95 pbk
	Taken for Pearls	poetry	£5.95 pbk
	War Voices	poetry	£5.95 pbk
John Davies	*Flight Patterns*	poetry	£5.95 pbk
	The Visitors' Book	fiction	£3.95 pbk
Christine Evans	*Cometary Phases*	poetry	£4.95 pbk
	Island of Dark Horses	poetry	£5.95 pbk
Catherine Fisher	*Immrama*	poetry	£3.95 pbk
	The Unexplored Ocean	poetry	£5.95 pbk
Paul Henry	*Time Pieces*	poetry	£5.95 pbk
Mike Jenkins	*A Dissident Voice*	poetry	£4.95 pbk
	Invisible Times	poetry	£3.95 pbk
	This House, My Ghetto	poetry	£5.95 pbk
Robert Minhinnick	*The Looters*	poetry	£4.95 pbk
	Hey Fatman	poetry	£5.95 pbk
Leslie Norris	*A Sea in the Desert*	poetry	£4.95 pbk
	Collected Poems		£8.95 pbk
	Girl from Cardigan	fiction	£9.95 hbk
	Collected Stories		£8.95 pbk
Sheenagh Pugh	*Beware Falling Tortoises*	poetry	£3.95 pbk
	Prisoners of Transience	trans.	£4.95 pbk
	Selected Poems	poetry	£5.95 pbk
	Sing for the Taxman	poetry	£5.95 pbk
Hilary Llewellyn-Williams	*Book of Shadows*	poetry	£5.95 pbk

For a catalogue of Seren titles, please write to Seren at 2 Wyndham Street, Bridgend, Mid Glamorgan, CF31 1EF. The above titles are available from good bookshops or direct from Seren. Orders should be accompanied by 75 pence postage and packing, with cheques made payable to Seren.